"Kat."

Her head cam glare. "I don't Katherine or i

"You were married?" That shouldn't have surprised him.

Her eyes were a brighter green than he remembered. The green of new leaves in springtime. A silver clip held her wavy auburn hair back from her face. The look would have been severe on another woman. On her, it emphasized the sculpted roundness of her cheekbones and her straight nose. Her full lower lip glistened. She wore a navy suit cut to follow her curves and accent her narrow waist. Her matching leather heels put the top of her head even with his shoulder. She was beautiful. A man would be insane to let her go.

"Adopted." She took Stevie's hand and started out of the room.

"What?" He'd lost himself in the sight of her, her answer slow to register.

"I was adopted after…" Her gaze dropped to the floor then rose to meet his with a cold, hard flash of defiance.

"I was adopted by a wonderful, kind woman named Alice. I took her name. Kat Jenkins doesn't exist anymore."

KD FLEMING

enjoys using stories of faith to share hope in her inspirational romances. She worked as a cashier, bank teller, traffic clerk (within a publishing company—don't ask), licensed insurance adjuster, and an accounts receivable and payroll coordinator before realizing she had the heart of a storyteller. Once she dared to imagine "what if," her life was changed forever.

She lives in a small town in west central Florida with her wonderful husband of fifteen years. They enjoy gardening, fishing, watching college football and basketball, and Caribbean cruises whenever KD isn't creating new stories or reading for her three amazing critique partners. She loves hearing from her readers and learning what helps them hold on to their faith and not lose hope. Visit KD at www.kdfleming.com.

KD FLEMING

Campaigning for Love

HEARTSONG
PRESENTS

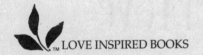

LOVE INSPIRED BOOKS

ISBN-13: 978-0-373-48727-1

CAMPAIGNING FOR LOVE

And be ye kind one to another, tenderhearted,
forgiving one another, even as God for Christ's sake
hath forgiven you.
—*Ephesians* 4:32

Thank you to my wonderful husband, Frank.
You never questioned this drive to write,
you just believed I could. I love you more!

My critique partners—
Carol Post, Sabrina Jarema and Dixie Taylor—
thank you for your honest and priceless feedback.
Your input is the ladder I climbed to get here. But
most of all, thank you for being my dear, dear friends.
You're all beyond compare in my heart.

To my fabulous editor, Kathy Davis,
for believing in my stories. And to my
awesome agent, Nalini Akolekar, your faith in my
writing was a lifeline during a personally painful year.
Thank you for not only your representation
but also your friendship. You are the best!

To all my family for their pride and encouragement
throughout this amazing journey.
Your enthusiasm is the best present ever.

For Mom and Dad Fleming (Howard and Ruby),
the pain of losing you both is still new,
but you live on in our hearts. We all miss you.

And thank you, God,
for Your mercy and love that fills me
and helps me share Your goodness through my stories.

God's love to all.

Chapter 1

Stevie Mills tugged on Katherine Harper's sleeve and went for the pen in her hand. His restlessness kept her busy until the bailiff called the courtroom to order. She glanced across the aisle with a ready smile of welcome for the new family court attorney. But instant recognition of his dark hair and classic features stole the smile from her lips and the air from her lungs. *Please God, no. Anyone but him.*

The man turned toward her and froze, a yellow file folder clutched in his hand. Ties of a briefly shared past bound their gazes. The fast hitch of her breath was a discordant rhythm against the sluggish tick of the large clock mounted on the back wall.

Back in high school, his voice had been flat and cold as he explained how he had time only for the "right" people, the people important to his future. And a girl raised in foster care was so unimportant she simply disappeared into the far reaches of the county. The memory stirred the painful embers of disillusionment in her already burning heart. She was the last person Nick Delaney would ever expect to see slated as his equal in a court of law.

Stevie's squirming freed her from the magnetic pull of Nick's piercing gaze. She turned her attention back to the little boy with golden hair and caramel-colored eyes and helped him find his favorite crayon.

"Miss Harper," the judge began. "Are you sure you want to proceed today?"

Grateful for the judge's concern but unwilling to appear affected, Katherine rose, wetting her dry lips. "Yes, sir. Stevie and I are ready to continue." She took her seat before her shaky legs betrayed her weakness. The recent loss of her adoptive mother had her emotions raw, and Nick's arrival while she was emotionally defenseless had her worried. But her problems didn't—couldn't—matter right now. Stevie needed her focused on her job. His well-being was all that counted.

Judge Pierce looked toward Nick. "And you, sir, are…?"

Nick stood and faced the bench. "Good morning, Your Honor. I'm Nicholas Delaney, on loan from Judge Hawthorne for two months." His gaze slid to the side, taking in the curve of sharp cheekbones and a firm chin, all made less severe by the red-gold glints in Kat's auburn hair. "I'm very glad to be here." She flinched but didn't turn his way. The smile he offered the judge was as honest as his words.

Judge Pierce pinned him with as stern a glare as Judge Hawthorne had when she'd meted out his punishment. "I trust you learned your lesson with Hawthorne and I won't have to use further measures to keep you in line." The judge swiveled in his leather chair, switching his gaze to Kat. "Bring us up to date and state your motion, Miss Harper."

"Sir, Stevie's been at Hanover House for two weeks and has established a routine with Mrs. Potter. He begins grief-counseling sessions Friday. A change in location now would offset the progress he's made adjusting to his situation. As his advocate, I recommend he remain at Hanover House until his grandmother is released from the hospital."

"Mr. Delaney, any thoughts on Miss Harper's recommendation?"

The use of Harper as her surname had Nick's gaze searching her left hand. She watched him, her face void of emotion. Her current poise and carriage at odds with his memory of the shy, hesitant girl who had befriended him in study hall thirteen years ago. This new Kat was a complete stranger. Yet he couldn't resist the lure that kept drawing him toward her.

With a forced effort, he looked down at his notes. "Actually, sir, I wondered why the minor was not..." A dull thud accompanied the rap of the judge's gavel and Nick's words faded.

"Mr. Delaney, we do not *ever* refer to a child in my courtroom by anything other than his or her name. They may be underage, but they most definitely are people and you will respect them as such."

"Of course, sir. I'm sorry." He looked first at the judge before nodding a silent apology toward Kat and Stevie.

"Why wasn't Stevie placed at a site closer to the hospital so arrangements could be made for him to visit his grandmother more often? Maybe we should consider doing that now, before he gets any more established in his current routine?"

The judge smiled at Kat while twirling his pen between his fingers. He leaned forward, as if eager for her response.

"Stevie is at Hanover House under Mrs. Potter's care because of her success in dealing with children who've suffered the loss of one or both parents." She kept her voice modulated to a tone as soothing as the hand she rubbed along Stevie's back.

"He sees his grandmother every other weekday and on Saturday and Sunday. When she's moved to the rehab center she'll be closer to Stevie's current location." She turned toward him with a raised eyebrow, all but daring him to say more.

"Forgive me." He resisted the urge to bow in deference to her imperialness. "I've had Stevie's case file for less than a week. I'm not up to speed on every aspect yet. I agree with choosing Hanover House as the—" He caught himself in time. "As Stevie's temporary residence. But what service drives him to the hospital on weekends?" He struggled to keep the censure out of his voice over a service that probably cost the state an arm and a leg.

Temper sparked in her eyes. "*I* drive Stevie on the weekends. We stop at his favorite restaurant on our way back. *My* treat."

He nodded, ceding her the point. The last thing he needed was to offend Kat and have the judge choose sides against him on his first day in family court.

Judge Pierce's voice broke the tense silence growing between them. "Do you have any other concerns in regard to this case, Mr. Delaney?"

"No, sir. I'm in full agreement with Miss Jenkins, I mean, Mrs. Harper's choices."

"Good, then this hearing is complete. Miss Harper, copy Mr. Delaney on the weekly progress reports you send to my office from now on." *Thunk* went the gavel.

"Yes, Your Honor. Thank you, Your Honor," they both said.

As Kat stuffed a file folder into her briefcase along with the coloring book and crayons she'd given Stevie earlier, Nick stepped toward her. He left his own paperwork spread across the table, forgotten for the moment.

"Kat."

Her head came up and she nailed him with a frigid glare. "I don't use that name anymore. Call me either Katherine or Miss Harper."

"You were married?" That shouldn't have surprised him. Her eyes were a brighter green than he remembered. The green of new leaves in springtime. A silver clip held her wavy auburn hair back from her face. The look would have been severe on another woman. On her, it emphasized the sculpted roundness of her cheekbones and her straight nose. Her full lower lip glistened from some clear cosmetic. She wore a navy suit cut to follow her curves and accent her narrow waist. Her matching leather heels put the top of her head even with his shoulder. She was beautiful. A man would be insane to let her go.

"Adopted." She took Stevie's hand and started out of the room.

"What?" He'd lost himself in the sight of her, her answer slow to register.

She stopped and pivoted to face him. "I was adopted after…" Her gaze dropped to the floor, then rose to meet his with a cold, hard flash of defiance. "I was adopted by a wonderful, kind woman named Alice. I took her name. Kat Jenkins doesn't exist anymore." She bent and whispered to Stevie before they walked away.

Nick stood motionless, staring after them. He'd wondered where she'd gone, if she'd been okay after she transferred. When he'd asked his father about her disappearance, he'd said it was common for kids like her, the ones who'd been in the system for years, to move on. They had no focus, no discipline. No sense of worth. They knew their future was doomed, and they were jealous of those more fortunate, so they disappeared.

Obviously, Kat, or Katherine as she preferred to be called, had found her focus. He marveled at her success. She was an attorney. She'd been better than he had been at math in high school. Thanks to her, he'd earned his acceptance into his father's alma mater based on his abilities, not his father's name.

He wasn't sure why God had sent him on this side trip through family court, but he would use the opportunity to renew his friendship with Katherine. She challenged him. Made him think beyond himself. To look for what others needed that he could provide. She didn't settle. He liked that about her. In a way, he had her to thank for his pursuing a career in politics. For wanting to give back. He collected his papers with a lighter heart than he'd had when his day had started. This was his second chance.

After court, Katherine dropped Stevie at Hanover House. Her heart was still pounding like a jackhammer as she drove to her office. Her short, angry gasps of breath, the thud of her heart slamming against her ribs, were a result of shock. Anyone would react this way if faced with someone from their past—someone who had betrayed them. There was no other explanation for the burning, tearing pain in her chest. A ghost from her past, piled on top of Alice's death, weighed her down with grief, making every breath a battle.

She rubbed her chest, trying to ease the pressure that had cinched tight around her the moment their eyes met. The sensation had nothing to do with Nick's handsome appearance. And it definitely had nothing to do with eyes the color of the deep sea. Because no matter how good he looked on the outside with his chiseled jaw and broad shoulders, inside beat the heart of a deceitful manipulator who used people for his own gain.

Nick wasn't thinking about what Stevie needed. His concern was for whatever closed the case faster so he could get back to his "billable hours" cases. Even if that meant separating Stevie and his grammy. But she wouldn't let him. Stevie and Mrs. Tindle had something sacred. They were a family.

Family. She beat back the urge to cry over her loss and squared her shoulders. All crying would do was give her a bigger headache. No one could claim she wasn't practical. *Detached*. The word drifted in the air around her.

Gina Lawson, her assistant, glanced up from her desk. The usual sparkle in her mischievous eyes dimmed when she spotted Katherine. She hopped up from her seat. "I thought you'd grab lunch at the courthouse. I'll fix some tea and order a salad from Ramon's," she said before heading to their small kitchenette.

She disappeared before Katherine could stop her. Gina believed her grandmother's secret brew could fix anything. Katherine grimaced and her tongue grew thick at the memory of the syrupy fix-all.

A few minutes later, a steaming cup of the amazing elixir sat on her desk. Gina stood behind her like a sentry assigned guard duty until every drop of the sweet, minty concoction was gone. In a gentle tone, Gina asked, "How are you holding up? Do you want me to call and reschedule the afternoon session?"

"I'm fine, just tired. We have a new attorney for the state. Things took longer than usual." She shifted the mountain of files on her desk and breathed through her nose, desperate to stifle the nausea swirling in her stomach.

"No one will think less of you if you stop giving your whole life to your job. No one expects that but you. You should take time for yourself."

"I had plenty of 'me' time last week. This is where I belong."

She'd grown up like the kids in these file folders, carried along through a system as bumpy and unfeeling as a conveyor belt. The constant shuffling kept emotional attachments at a minimum. *Safe.*

She shut her eyes against the bitter acceptance that her purpose in life was as a temporary part of someone else's, a sort of stopgap before they moved on. The ugly truth was she wasn't meant for the permanence of a family.

Gina sat facing her. "You deserve a husband, a family, not an ever-changing array of faces in file folders. Jeremy just preached on this."

Jeremy, her pastor, preached monthly about how God didn't intend for people to be alone, citing Adam and Eve as the first example. He claimed God allows special people into our lives for companionship. A parent, a friend or—through the natural progression of relationships—a soul mate.

But Katherine knew better. She was the exception to the rule. Friend? She'd thought she'd found one in Nick a long time ago. Parent? She'd had two—no, three. Her birth parents were dead, and now, so was Alice. She wasn't about to think of the damage a professed soul mate could inflict on her banged-up heart. The mere idea had her vowing to roll the fragile organ in a triple layer of bubble wrap and stick it on a shelf well out of reach forever.

She swallowed against the constriction in her throat and held tight to her resolve when she answered Gina. "I gave up on fairy tales and Prince Charming a long time ago. I have a lot to do. If there isn't anything else, I need some quiet time before I have to go back." Her gaze moved to the files.

"Well." Gina wouldn't meet her eyes. "You know the list of your volunteer work Judge Pierce wanted turned in for the community service selection committee? His clerk called this morning to remind me of the deadline."

The pulses of pain throbbing in her head morphed into

thorns of irritation, and her words came out with a definite bite. "I'm not interested in becoming Pemberly's next Citizen of the Year. The selection committee uses the responses from the volunteer list to nominate candidates for the award. I'm busy doing real work in the real world. I'm a paid officer of the court. It's wrong to reward me for doing my job."

Gina harrumphed and waved the form at her. "I filled it out for you. All you have to do is sign right here." She jabbed her finger at the red sticky tab marking the spot. "And, Ms. Paid Officer of the Court, I don't recall you getting any compensation for the nights, weekends or holidays you spend at the shelters and halfway houses giving out free legal advice." She paused only long enough to breathe. "Not to mention, driving a little boy to see his grandmother while she's in the hospital. If anyone deserves an award for looking out for this community, it's you. And while you're at it, why don't you think about running for public office? I heard there's a seat open on the city council."

Couldn't she catch a break today? Her body ached as if they'd all used it as a punching bag. The tea hadn't worked its special effects. Her head was still pounding. "I told you, I'm not signing it. Now let it go." In one fluid motion, she plucked the paper out of Gina's hand, wadded it up, and tossed it toward the garbage can.

Gina's look as she salvaged her reusable sticky tab from the crumpled paper conveyed her belief Katherine had lost her mind. "I'm telling Judge Pierce you're being stubborn. And, I made copies. Lots of copies." She stalked back to her desk.

"I'm always stubborn. That's how I get my way in court," she yelled toward the empty doorway. With a tired sigh, she rubbed at the ache in her temples and prayed she was wrong about God's plan for her life.

Chapter 2

Katherine breathed a silent thank-you when Judge Pierce tapped his gavel at the conclusion of the afternoon session.

"Miss Harper, my clerk requested some paperwork from you. Your assistant believes it will be turned in late."

She closed her eyes and bit her lower lip. "I'm sorry. It's just that..." She heaved a weary sigh but straightened her spine, ready to argue. "I can't see how it's necessary to complete the paperwork at this time. There are plenty of other members in the community who are more deserving of the committee's consideration." She held her breath and prayed in silence.

"You know I'm on the selection committee this year." The judge's voice held an inflexible edge.

"I know. But I'm asking you to—" She would not beg. "Pick someone else this year." She struggled to keep the sheen of tears from her eyes. She was counting on him remembering his offer of a continuance this morning. She hated pity. But she hated drawing attention to herself even more. And this ridiculous idea of nominating her for Citizen of the Year screamed, "Hey, look at me!" for sure.

He folded his arms across his chest. "Each judge sponsors a candidate. I chose you. I want those papers completed and on my desk within the next week, young lady, or I'll hold you in contempt!" He rapped his gavel with enough force the block jumped. He rose and strode out of the courtroom as regal as a prince.

She gaped at his display of temper.

"What was that all about?" Nick asked.

She snapped her briefcase closed. "It's personal."

"Yeah, judges ask about paperwork that's personal while on the bench." His voice dripped sarcasm.

"It has nothing to do with the court. He and a bunch of his judicial friends serve on the board. He can make me talk about it here, but he can't use the bench to force me to do what he wants."

He shrugged. "All my cases are processed at the courthouse downtown. I'm not too familiar with the annex. Is there a place around here that serves a good cup of coffee?"

She grabbed her briefcase, ready to leave. "There's a cafeteria on the ground floor. Sorry, I'm late. I'll see you back here Tuesday."

Nick was blocking her path of escape. He held her gaze for a stalled heartbeat, and then moved aside. "I'll catch you next time."

Nick sat across from his father in the country club dining room. The gurgle of water trickling over the rocks in the fountain nearby muted the clink of silverware and glass. They had dinner here every Thursday night. His father used the meal to push whatever agenda he had in mind for Nick's future.

"How is family court going?" Edward Delaney asked.

"Nothing like civil court. Those kids' stories will tear your heart out. The advocate serving with Judge Pierce is great. She's very involved in their lives and cares about what happens to them."

His dad let out a long sigh, waiting until the waiter left. "You need to focus on your image and link yourself with people who can boost your political career."

Nick's appetite faded the longer his father spoke.

"Abby Blackmon is single. She's an attorney and her father is a U.S. senator. You'd have a lot in common." He punctuated his words with jabs of his fork. "The Citizen of the Year dinner is coming up. I left a pair of tickets with your secretary. The press will be there photographing the who's who of the city. A picture in the paper with Abby Blackmon on your arm would show the citizens of Pemberly you're friends with the right kind of people. Powerful people."

Nick's worst nightmare had come true. His father intended to pick his wife out for him. He took a drink of water to moisten his dry throat. "I appreciate your concern and your warnings, Dad, but I'll find my own date. And, I'll pick my own wife, if I get married."

"If? Look here, boy…" His father dropped his voice when the couple at the next table stared at them. "Do you know how hard it is to get elected if you're single? Voters associate marriage with stability, with commitment."

"Maybe so, but I won't choose my wife based on her pedigree. Or what she can do for my career, political or otherwise. I want someone who loves me for myself. Someone who makes me happy. Besides, you never remarried."

A flash of pain so brief he could have imaged it crossed his father's face, chased away by a belligerent growl.

Nick regretted the remarriage comment and drew the conversation back to his father's favorite topic with a confident grin. "Besides, I have an election to win. I don't have time for a personal life these days. But if I did, I'd find my own date to the dinner." The image of green eyes sparking with temper from across the courtroom stole into his mind.

His father's jaw flexed. But the determined edge in Nick's voice held him in check. Their biggest disagreements revolved around women. Their difference of opinion had surfaced when Nick was in high school. His father had encouraged him to date girls from prominent families. But if someone's lineage hadn't measured up to his father's high standards, he'd hounded Nick until it was impossible to continue any type of contact. There would be a fight when his father discovered Katherine Harper, the attorney, was Kat Jenkins, former foster kid.

"You can't afford any distractions, not when you're this close to the first big step in your political career. I'd give anything to trade places with you. To have the opportunities you have available for your future."

Edward Delaney's favorite words. Nick managed not to roll his eyes. Anytime he hesitated about going along with his father's vision, out came those words. He understood his father's drive. Respected it, and even accepted it—most of the time. He wanted to tell his father that he could receive as many blessings for himself if he opened his heart to Christ. His father wouldn't receive the words the way he intended them. Instead, he would mock Nick's faith.

Despite the grief his father would give him, Nick wanted to renew his friendship with Katherine. To get to know her, find out why she'd run away, and what had made her decide to practice law. He hoped that maybe all his talk about law school had influenced her career choice. He was so glad their paths had crossed. That it had happened at all just proved God's continued blessings on his life.

By the next day, Nick questioned his optimism. Unavailable, again. How could she be out of the office every time he called? He'd left several messages with her assistant. The woman sounded polite, but after the second call, he knew Kat was there. The ever-efficient Gina stumbled over an

excuse instead of putting him through. He tried her cell.
Four rings, then voicemail. He just wanted to talk to her
without a three-foot-tall munchkin present.

It was almost lunchtime before Katherine came into the
office Monday. While she was out, Gina had papered her
desk with phone messages. One was from Nick with the
notation "personal" checked. She wadded up the blue strip
of paper and aimed for the trash.

Gina ordered lunch in and they went over progress reports due to the court for each of the children assigned to
her office.

The conference room phone rang. Gina reached for the
handset. "Katherine Harper's office. Yes, she is. May I ask
who is calling?" Gina pressed the hold button. "It's Nick
Delaney. I put a message from him on your desk."

Katherine kept her eyes on the pages in front of her. "Tell
him I'm unavailable." She ignored the growing silence that
spread between them.

"I'm sorry, sir, but Miss Harper is unavailable. Yes, I
would be happy to let her know you called. Thank you,
goodbye."

After Gina hung up, she leaned across the table. "What
gives?"

They'd worked together for five years and they were
friends. Gina's brazenness meant Katherine's personal life
was as open for discussion as the files laid out in front of
them.

Katherine avoided direct eye contact. "Nothing, he's
the attorney for the state. We don't have any issues that he
needs to discuss with me, and I'm busy. I don't have time
for small talk."

"How do you know it's small talk?" Gina's eyes widened. "Wait. Is he *the* Nicholas Delaney, heir to the Ed-

ward Delaney corporate attorney mega firm?" Her voice
went all breathy and she wiggled her eyebrows in a very
bad Groucho Marx imitation.

"Yes, *he* is." There was no telling where this conversation would go after she admitted that piece of information.

"How'd he end up in family court?"

"Judge Hawthorne cited him for contempt. He's serving out a two-month sentence." She gathered up the files
on the table, intent on making her escape. She'd finish her
work in her office. Across the hall. Away from Gina. And
avoid further talk about Nick.

"Realllly?"

The way Gina strung the word out didn't bode well for
a speedy exit. Katherine shot her an impatient glare, which
Gina ignored.

"I bet Daddy's furious over the timing of this little side
trip."

Already regretting feeding Gina's penchant for gossip,
the words tumbled out of Katherine's mouth. "What are
you talking about?"

With a very pleased smile, Gina spilled. "The chatter at
lunch among us lowly assistants is that Daddy wants Nicky
Boy to run for city council. He's expected to go public with
his announcement any day now."

The words stalled Katherine in the doorway. "I guess
he'll get his wish," she said more to herself than Gina before going into her office and closing the door.

Her cell phone rang. Nick's number popped up on the
display. She pressed "ignore" and set the phone face down
on her desk. He'd figure out not everyone jumped when a
Delaney beckoned.

Tuesday morning, Nick stood waiting outside the courtroom twenty minutes before the start of session. Katherine

came out of the elevator holding a little girl's hand. They stopped outside the restroom. She leaned down and spoke to the little girl before she went inside. Alone.

He walked up behind her. "Katherine."

She spun around, her eyes wide, her hand over her heart. "Oh, Nick, you startled me."

"Sorry. You are one busy lady. I've been calling you since Saturday and haven't been able to reach you."

"Was there a case we needed to discuss?"

No admission of avoiding him, but she didn't meet his gaze. "I wondered if you had time to talk. Catch up on what's been going on since high school." No need to tip his hand or scare her away, but he needed more than two minutes outside the courtroom to do this right. They could be setting the foundation for the renewal of their friendship.

His confidence in his plan wavered as her expression morphed from wary to cool then outright angry, leaving her cheeks tinged with pink and her nostrils flaring.

"Catch up on old times?" Her voice took on a frosty edge. "There's nothing to catch up on."

The little girl came out of the ladies' room and wrapped her arms around Katherine's leg. She reached down and smoothed her dark hair. "We have to get going. I wouldn't want to be late. Judge Pierce doesn't cite contempt very often, but he is touchy about tardiness."

"So I've heard." He followed them into the courtroom.

"Just be honest with me." He spoke to her back as she settled Susan into the booster seat. "Why won't you take my calls?"

She shot a quick glance at him before she pulled a princess coloring book and crayons from her briefcase. "We don't have anything personal to say to each other. It's not like we were friends."

"Are you kidding me?" They'd spent hours in the library

after school, not just solving calculus problems, but arguing about pizza, discussing the latest movie or talking about music or books they'd read. Where was this coming from? What had turned her against him?

And of course, Judge Pierce chose that moment to walk in and take his seat.

Unable to hide his growing frustration, Nick dropped his voice to a harsh whisper. "Come on, Kat, we need to talk."

"Don't call me that! She doesn't exist. I don't have time to talk to you, and I don't want to." She spat the words at him.

"Miss Harper and Susan, it's good to see you this morning. You too, Mr. Delaney." The judge greeted them.

"Thank you, Your Honor," they both said.

Katherine gave background on Susan's case and made her recommendations. But Nick had studied Susan's file. He presented alternate housing and placement solutions and questioned her recommendations. Apparently, the "Unreachable Katherine Harper" didn't like having her choices questioned. Well, she'd see he took his job as the state's representative as seriously as she took her position as the child's advocate.

"What are you doing?" She hissed after his latest counter-suggestion.

"My job. That's why I'm here."

"You don't have a job here. You're doing penance!"

The venom in her voice had him jerking his head around to face her. "Maybe so, but I care about these kids just as much as you do."

The derisive roll of her eyes had him praying for patience.

The insistent tapping of the gavel forced Katherine's gaze away from Nick in time to catch the frown on Judge Pierce's face. Great. What had she missed?

She followed the judge's gaze toward Susan. The little girl had her doll clutched to her chest. Her lower lip was quivering and her big blue eyes sparkled with unshed tears.

Burning shame washed over Katherine. She scooted over and pulled Susan into her lap, cradling her in her arms. "Oh sweetie, I'm so sorry. I didn't mean to upset you. It's okay. Everything is fine."

She glared at Nick, who at least had the decency to look shamefaced.

Disgust rolled within her for losing sight of what was most important and upsetting this sweet little girl. "I'm so sorry, Your Honor. I don't know what came over me. I lost my focus. I won't let it happen again."

"Your Honor, it was my fault," Nick interrupted. "I tried to speak with Miss Harper about something that could have waited until after session. I apologize for distracting her and disrupting your courtroom."

His attempt to deflect blame away from her was unexpected. She glanced over at him before she looked back at the judge.

The judge watched both of them, his eyes searching, assessing, before he spoke. "Bailiff, please bring Mrs. Davis in and ask her to take Susan back to Trinity Care. We're finished with her hearing for today. Miss Harper, you and Mr. Delaney meet me in my chambers in ten minutes." *Bam!*

They both jumped.

Katherine ignored Nick. She didn't answer him when he called after her on the way down the long hall to Judge Pierce's office. She walked as fast as she could without breaking into a full sprint, putting as much distance between them as possible.

That scene in the courtroom. She'd never been so out of control. Forgetting what she was doing. The child's welfare came ahead of everything else—always. She'd been so engrossed in taking Nick down a peg, she'd forgotten where she was, what mattered most. She'd forgotten about Susan.

"Kat. Katherine, wait. Talk to me. Why are you so upset?" He was gaining on her.

She paused in front of the judge's door and let him catch up. "My life has been just fine for the past thirteen years without you in it." She took a deep breath. "I don't see any reason to change that. What could we have to say to each other after all this time? I mean, seriously, Nick?"

Before he could respond, the door swung open.

"Come in, Katherine, Nick. Take a seat."

Once they were inside, Judge Pierce pinned both of them with a heated glower. "Would someone like to explain to me what just happened in my courtroom?"

"Well…"

"You see…"

He held up a hand. "One at a time, please. Better yet, I'll start. Do you two know each other?"

She looked at Nick, unable to keep her temper from flaring. "We, um, we went to the same high school for part of a semester our senior year. We haven't seen each other since then. Not until last week in your courtroom."

"I see. Were you friends?"

"Not really. We had a class together. I—I was only there for a short time. We didn't get a chance to know each other. We moved in different circles."

"Anything you want to add to Miss Harper's version, Mr. Delaney?"

"We barely knew each other." He kept his eyes diverted.

"And yet here both of you are, attorneys in the same court of law. Am I the only one who finds this an odd twist of fate?"

"I'm afraid I don't know what you mean," Nick said.

"Only an observation, young man." The judge leaned

forward, bouncing his gaze between them. "The two of you seem to need a place to discuss things aside from my courtroom and out of the presence of a child. Why don't I make a suggestion? How about lunch?"

"Judge Pierce, please. I have a backlog of cases to review. I don't have the time…" Out of the corner of her eye, she took in the firm set of Nick's jaw. "Or the inclination to speak with Mr. Delaney outside the courtroom."

Nick turned to face her, his eyes darker than indigo. "It is clear Kat—I mean, Katherine—can only tolerate speaking with me in court, Your Honor. So I'll apologize for trying to compel her into doing otherwise and limit my interactions with her to court business."

"All right, children, I've had enough."

Both their gazes flew to him.

"The two of you leave me no choice. You think this is a game. That you can push and get your way while shooting daggers at each other with your eyes during session in *my* courtroom. I will not allow it. Especially in front of an innocent child. This ends today. Mr. Delaney, do you cook?"

"Excuse me?"

"Do you cook? It's a simple enough question."

"I can boil water."

"Well then, the food will fall to Miss Harper, and you will assist."

The judge's words left her wide-eyed and stunned.

"Your Honor, sir…please don't." A sickening dread crept up from her stomach to clog her throat. She'd beg if she had to. Anything but what she was afraid he was going to make her do.

He gave her a hard look. "This Friday is a holiday. We have a long weekend ahead of us. You and Mr. Delaney will spend the long weekend with me. Melvia is out of town visiting the grandchildren, and I'll be home alone. The three of us will spend quality time together getting to know each other." He leaned back, folded his arms over his chest, and smiled with smug satisfaction.

She stared at him, her mouth wide open and her jaw slack. When she risked a glance at Nick, his head was swiveling between her and the judge. She would not feel guilty about their predicament. This was his fault. Not hers.

The judge continued to smile. The clock ticked away the seconds for an endless minute before she recovered enough to speak. "Judge Pierce, Uncle Charles…"

Her familial reference propelled Nick out of his chair. He paced the room. Torn between demanding an explanation about her relationship with the judge and using this weekend to make her face him and explain. Her denial clashed with his dread of being the subject of judicial displeasure, again. And all because of a harmless conversation that wouldn't have mattered in the grand scheme of things, if he'd timed it better. He'd wanted to know what had happened to her after she transferred.

This was unbelievable, laughable even. Oh, he wanted to say something. To yell and scream about the downward spiral his family court experience was having on his ready-to-launch political career. But when his eyes met hers, he ground his teeth and turned to look out the window. Fragile, vulnerable, beaten. They were the only words to describe the weighted hunch of her shoulders and the stricken look on her face.

Just like that day in the library thirteen years ago. Her emotions were on display, like a marquee on Broadway for anyone to read. The mask she wore in the courtroom ripped away.

"Uncle Charles, you know I have responsibilities this

weekend. Stevie Mills is one of them. I can't abandon him. How will he see his grammy?"

The panic in her voice tore at Nick. They needed a way out of the insanity his quest to renew their friendship had caused. But his mind was blank. He couldn't offer one single, logical solution that would get them out of this mess.

"Don't worry, I'm sure Mrs. Potter will be more than happy to shuttle Stevie to the rehab center since it's so close by. And I'll check with Gina. She'd love the chance to take your place with Jeremy on Friday night. That leaves Saturday and Sunday. Even the Lord rested on Sunday, young lady."

Nick turned. "Who's Jeremy?"

She notched her chin. "A man's name is all you got out of the conversation? Typical."

"There's nothing typical about this conversation! Not by a long shot, sweetheart. Judge Pierce, sir, I don't know what's going on here, but I think I'm entitled to an explanation." He leaned against the wall beside the window and leveled his hard gaze on the judge.

"I'd be honored—no pun intended." The judge smiled before he took on a serious mien. "You and Katherine are going to spend the weekend with me, at my home. We'll have breakfast, lunch and dinner together. The two of you will spend one hour in the morning, afternoon, and evening together, where you will converse. Both of you will have to share something you learned about each other with me while we enjoy the meal you will prepare—together.

"Katherine, you will cook. Nick, you'll assist her, and I do mean assist. If she says chop, you chop. If she says stir, you stir. We will enjoy this time together, and there will be no fighting, or both of you will find yourselves enjoying this city's finest hospitality behind bars come Monday morning. Do I make myself clear?"

"I don't understand." The confusion flavoring Katherine's words today sounded the same as it had all those years ago when Nick had laid out his father's plans for his future, and knotted his stomach just as tight now as it had then.

The judge's tone carried a hard edge that clashed with the concerned look he sent her way. "Since you and Mr. Delaney feel the need to act like teenagers in my courtroom, consider yourselves in time-out, or on restriction, whichever you prefer. Katherine, have Gina provide Mr. Delaney's office with your home address. He will pick you up at five on Friday afternoon. I'll have the refrigerator stocked so you can come straight there."

The judge made eye contact with both of them, his look of concern gone. "I've cancelled tomorrow's session so the two of you can tie up any loose ends before our happy weekend together. Off you go now." He motioned toward the door with his hand in a careless wave.

A speechless Katherine and Nick walked out of his office.

Nick reached toward her after the door closed behind them. "Kat, I—"

"Don't! Don't even try. There is nothing you can say right now that I want to hear."

Chapter 3

Katherine stormed through the glass doors of her office suite and flung her briefcase at the nearest chair. The hairpins anchoring her French twist were her next victims. She unleashed an angry growl and shook her head, torpedoing the area with any last holdouts.

Gina ended her phone call and quirked her brow at Katherine's uncharacteristic bout of temper. "Bad day in court?" Then jumped back when a stray pin bounced off her monitor.

"That man...he...he...he's ruining my life! Why couldn't he let it go? When I didn't take his calls on my cell phone, you'd think he'd get the clue that I do not want to speak to him! Arrgh!" She raged more to herself than Gina, pacing off the perimeter of the room like an angry bear.

"I'll be right back." Gina scooted out from behind her desk and headed down the hall at a fast clip. She returned with a cup of tea, but hung back until Katherine reined her temper in enough that she stopped gesturing wildly with her hands.

When a cough that sounded a lot like a chuckle escaped from her assistant's mouth, Katherine leveled a squinted glare on her. "It's not funny."

"Does this have to do with a certain Mr. Nicholas Delaney, by any chance?" Gina eased within arm's reach, placing the cup on the counter in front of Katherine like an offering to a vengeful overlord.

With a deep, slow breath, she collected herself before reaching for the piece of flowery china. It was that or hurl the cup against the wall. "Yes. He and I had a fight during session today." She plopped into a chair. "As our punishment, Judge Pierce has ordered us to spend the weekend..." She shuddered. "All weekend together. We have to share three meals a day, which I have to cook with Nick as my helper. The man's culinary skills start and stop with boiled water. And I don't know if that's on the stove or in the microwave."

Another laugh escaped. Gina gave her an apologetic shrug that made Katherine want to scream.

"The whole weekend, huh?" Gina nodded her head. "Now I understand why the judge wanted me to fill in for you with Jeremy at Grace Community Friday night."

"Judge Pierce wants us to have time to talk to each other about non-court-related subjects, and the only way to ensure I'll cooperate is by holding me hostage at his house— where he can keep an eye on me!" Katherine gnashed her teeth and tapped her nails against the solid surface of the counter, desperate for a way around the judge's orders. An idea started forming in her head. *Oh, yeah.* But could she? There was no question. *Definitely.*

She smiled at her own cleverness. "Gina. My dear, wonderful and resourceful Gina. How about using your super sleuth skills and getting me every known fact on Mr. Nicholas Delaney, attorney-at-law?" She let out a pleased sigh. "If Uncle Charles wants a mini-bio on Nick at each meal, he'll get one. I just won't use Nicky Boy as my source."

She headed toward her office with a bounce in her step. She'd won round one.

Her sense of victory was short-lived. In the silence of her office, there was nothing to keep the memories of her last personal conversation with Nick at bay. With her emotions churning, suddenly thirteen years ago was as vivid as yesterday. The scars from the old wounds Nick had inflicted with his betrayal reopened. All his talk about how important knowing the right people would be to his future. The doors those right people could open for him. She'd faked a smile and prayed she could hold her tears inside until later. What had he expected her to say? He'd told her things for him were moving fast. His summer wasn't his. He was leaving for college the day after graduation. He'd said he'd be too busy to see her, much less call. She'd been sad for herself—she was losing her only friend—but she'd been happy for him. He had a chance at realizing his dream. At that point, she hadn't had an inkling of a dream.

She didn't fit into his world of "the right people." Honestly, where would a connection with a poor orphan living in a children's home get him? But he hadn't given her the chance to bow out, to set him free. He'd treated her like an ugly secret no one could ever know about.

He'd said his father was an attorney. Told her he handled some family services cases.

She knew he'd handled at least one.

Hers.

And Nick had gotten him to do it. To banish her to the most remote area in the district to finish out her senior year at a new school in a new group home. Among strangers.

No matter how deep she buried the memories, the slightest reminder of how gullible she'd been still infuriated her. If she hadn't been so alone, she would have known all his attention and charm were an act. Whoever heard of Prince Charming hanging out with Orphan Annie?

She sniffed, forbidding a single tear to pool, because the worst part, the part that shamed her the most, the part that still made her want to scream, was how desperate she'd been. So needy for a connection of any kind to anyone, she would have tutored him just for the company. There had been no need to pretend she mattered to him.

Nick had used her. And now Uncle Charles expected her to spend time with him, finding out personal, interesting things about the guy who had manipulated her and then banished her to the equivalent of Siberia.

She knew all she needed to know about Nicholas Delaney and none of it was interesting. A dull ache filled her chest as another piece of her heart shriveled up and died over the injustice of having to relive the past she'd worked so hard to escape.

Alice had taught her that her past was gone. She couldn't do a thing about it today. "Let it go," she always said. "Shake the dust off your feet and forget those naysayers. You have tomorrow to get ready for."

A smile tugged at her lips. Alice had never let her wallow in self-pity. She'd helped Katherine see how putting her faith and trust in God meant she didn't have to worry about pleasing anyone else. God's opinion was all that mattered.

Her body ached from the emotional havoc the judge had wreaked on her life today. Reviewing case files in her current mindset was useless. She gathered up the files to take home with her. She came out of her office and leaned on Gina's desk. "I've had enough, I'm leaving. Feel free to cut out early this afternoon. I'll see you in the morning."

Gina's head popped up from behind her monitor. "Are you sick?"

"No, just tired. I can't focus like I should right now."

The weight of her loss, the memories of her past, and Uncle Charles's strong-arming rode heavy on her shoulders. "I thought I'd swing by Grace Community and explain to Jeremy why I'm bailing on him Friday."

"Go home, fill the tub with bubbles and relax." Gina waved her off. "You work too hard. You haven't given yourself any downtime since losing Alice. You need to let your mind rest and your heart heal."

Katherine paused in the middle of sliding her purse strap onto her shoulder. "I said I was tired. I don't remember any claims about being sad or mopey." She shook her head at Gina's raised eyebrow and relented—a little. "But a bubble bath does sound good. I'll see you in the morning." In the open doorway, she turned. "Get me the dirt on Nick Delaney."

Thanks to the light traffic, Katherine made good time on her way across town and pulled up beside Jeremy's car. Using the main entrance, she went through to the church office and tapped on his private door. He beckoned her in with a wave of his hand and a welcoming smile.

"Hey there, stranger." He stood and, when he was within arm's reach, claimed a big-brother hug. "What brings you by at this time of day?"

She hugged him back, welcoming his warmth, hoping it would reach deep enough to chase away the cold loneliness holding her soul hostage. "I decided to play hooky for the afternoon."

He stepped back and scanned her face. "Uh-huh, I see that. Anything going on you want to talk about?"

Her eyes widened. His ability to sense her mood was downright spooky sometimes. She shifted her gaze to a spot over his shoulder. "I'm fine."

He squeezed her hand. "Come on, Katherine, I know

you better than that. And it's a very bad thing to mislead your minister."

The internal war raging between unloading her burdens and keeping them locked inside lasted less than thirty seconds. She sank into a chair as her composure crumbled. Jeremy was safe. He'd been her first real friend. He wouldn't take advantage of her outward show of emotion, and if she could unload part of the weight, she could handle the rest—alone. Always alone. His look of devoted concern toppled the last of her weakened defenses.

Despite a soul-weary sigh, she fought against sounding like a whiney wimp. No pity. She needed advice from someone who knew her. Aside from Jeremy, there was only Uncle Charles and what he'd done to her was part of the problem.

"I'm having a bad life right now. There are a lot of things coming at me all at once, and—and I'm not feeling especially battle-ready today." She looked up, searching his face. For what, she didn't know, but she needed to fill the silence somehow. "How's that for honesty, *Pastor* Jeremy?"

He sat down next to her, took her hands in his, and held on. "It's pretty good for someone who has a phobia about admitting she gets overloaded. What's going on that's making you feel this way?"

"My past has found a way to resurrect itself and become part of my daily courtroom life." At his confused look, she elaborated, "A guy from one of the high schools I attended is serving in family court with me. He called me over the weekend. He's interested in playing catch-up with a part of my life I buried forever." She stared at their joined hands, drawing on his comfort. "I have nothing to say to him."

Too restless to sit, she got up and paced. There, she'd told him the important parts. Even Jeremy didn't need to know all the dirty details of why she didn't want to talk to

Nick. The silence around them grew while Jeremy waited her out. No pity. She hated pity. She didn't want anyone knowing how pathetic she'd been as a teenager, not even Jeremy. She appreciated his sympathy for her loss, but if he knew what Nick and his father had done to her, he'd feel sorry for her. She couldn't take that right now.

She turned and faced him. "Alice taught me the past—well—it belongs behind me. She said it was better to look ahead to where I'm going, not where I'd been." She hugged her arms about her body to stave off the icy chill of loneliness that settled over her.

Jeremy stood, but didn't infringe on her space. "Katherine, you've been hit with so much all at once. You're grieving the loss of your mother." When she tried to speak, he raised his hand and checked her protest. "I know she adopted you." His eyes, his words, were so earnest. "That woman couldn't have loved you any more if she'd given birth to you, and you loved her just as much. That's what made her your mom. Now, this trouble you're having at work. All of it combined would be too much for anyone."

She was helpless against the hot tears leaking from her eyes. She confessed in a jagged whisper, "I miss her so much. She'd know what to do about work and Uncle Charles and his crazy schemes." She wiped her face and moved away when he reached for her, unsure whether he was offering pity or comfort this time.

His voice turned heavy with protective intensity. "What has Judge Pierce done that's upset you? You're very special to him. He wouldn't make you do something he didn't think would help you."

Her nod was her only response.

"There's something I need to tell you." Jeremy turned her to face him. "I know about the Citizen of the Year nomination. I asked the judge if he'd apply some pressure and help me persuade you. Alice asked me to arrange your nomination for the award when I visited her in the hospital. Of course, I would have waited before putting my plan into action if I'd known you were so overwhelmed at work."

When she kept quiet, he went on. "All you're doing is documenting what you do all the time. This, in no way, means they'll select you and it's not bragging about what you do to help others. It's more like bearing witness to your spirit of giving."

Then he hit her with the ultimate low blow. "It was important enough to Alice that I promised her I'd make it happen. Don't fight the judge over this," he pleaded. "We all care about you." He smoothed the side of his finger along her jaw and caught a stray tear. "A lot. And we're proud of you and how you look out for people who don't have anyone else to stand up for them."

The intense silence was too much. "All right," she mumbled. She was so tired of fighting them on this. "I don't agree, but if I'd known this was so important to Alice, I wouldn't have balked."

The look on his face was doubtful at best.

"I wouldn't have balked, *as* much."

He smiled. "Feel better?"

After a long sigh, she said, "Yeah, I do. Thanks for loaning me your shoulder." She gently pushed her fist against his left shoulder.

"No problem, it's part of the job." He shrugged before his face turned somber. "You have to grieve over your loss before your heart can heal. You haven't had many people in your life that mattered to you, and she was the most special. Losing someone you love is painful for anyone, not just you." He shook his head. "This isn't anything I wouldn't say to someone else. But I'll be more insistent with you because I know how you keep your feelings bottled up inside. You can't heal until you've dealt with the pain. You've had enough heartache in your life. It's time you found some happiness."

"And you said I paid more attention than you in psych class?" She tried to tease him, welcoming the peace that seeped into her soul. She'd needed this. God had sent her here, to her refuge in the storm. To someone who would seek God's guidance and say the words her heart needed to hear.

With a small smile, she took his hands the way he'd held hers. "I'm not good at letting myself get attached to people, but you have to know I treasure our friendship. You mean a lot to me." She swallowed hard. "Thank you for always giving me a shelter when the forecast includes a hurricane."

After she accepted another crushing hug, she went home for the bubble bath Gina had recommended. And, she had a questionnaire about her volunteer work to fill out. Even though it was a waste of time. They didn't name do-gooder children's advocates Citizen of the Year.

"Oh my goodness! Is this the end of the world as I know it?" Gina snatched the completed *and* signed bio page Katherine had taped to her monitor. She disregarded the muffin and a coffee with a sticky note saying "thanks" that Katherine had left beside her keyboard and hurried into Katherine's office.

Katherine tried for an imitation of the cheeky grin she usually received after Gina got her way on something. "What?"

"Don't 'what' me," Gina scolded, standing in front of Katherine's desk with her hands on her hips. "You said you'd never fill this thing out, and now here it is, complete with your signature. What changed your mind?"

She worked at holding a straight face. "I guess the bubble bath relaxed me more than I expected."

Gina's response was a snort and a skeptical arch of her brow.

Katherine closed the file in front of her and met Gina's curious gaze. "I saw Jeremy yesterday and he said he asked the judge to help him convince me to submit the form. Alice asked him to do it. I couldn't live with myself if I didn't grant her final wish after everything she did for me." She had to force the last words past a sudden lump in her throat.

Gina came around the desk. "Mmmwahhh!" She dropped a smacking kiss on the top of Katherine's head. "I'm so proud of you. I know you didn't want to do this, but you did it anyway because it was important to someone else."

The ringing of the phone sent Gina hurrying back out to her desk. Between the open door of her office and Gina's booming voice, Katherine couldn't help but hear her. "Katherine Harper's office. Yes, she's in, Mr. Delaney. One moment please."

Knowing she was stuck spending the weekend with him and the judge, Katherine reached for the phone and pressed the flashing button. She ignored Gina's nosy presence at her door, listening to her side of the conversation.

"This is Katherine. Yes, that's how I answer the phone even if I know the caller." She didn't try to smooth the edge in her voice and ignored Gina's fingers prompting her to smile. "How may I help you? Sure, that's fine. Okay, I'll see you then. Goodbye."

Before the phone was back in the cradle, Gina claimed the chair facing her. "I made a file of his biggest accomplishments for you. But what did he want now?"

"He asked if he could pick me up a little early because he has an errand to run on the way to the judge's house."

"Are you still mad at him?"

Katherine drummed her fingers on her desk searching for an answer that wouldn't reveal how painful being around Nick was for her. No one knew the depth of hurt she'd experienced at the hands of Nick and his father, and she wasn't sure she could explain it. And she didn't want to, either. She tried so hard to be obedient to God's will for her life, but forgiving Nick was a lot harder than forgetting him. She had a long way to go to move past her animosity.

"I'm not sure mad is the right word. He's part of my past. A very brief part," she added. No need for Gina to read more into this pseudo-relationship than there was.

"I've worked hard at forgetting what my life was like before my adoption. Everything before Alice is a bad memory for me. By acknowledging Nick, I have to go back to a time that was painful for me, and I don't think I'm strong enough to deal with that right now. I like being in control of my environment because I wasn't in control of anything while I lived in foster care. Nick's presence makes me feel like some of that control is slipping from my grasp."

Gina listened without interruption while Katherine shared a tiny glimpse into the past she kept hidden from everyone. "I can't imagine what it was like for you growing up that way. I see you as you are now." Gina motioned to her with a sweep of her hand. "You're so accomplished, so focused on what is important. Your past may be painful for you, but be honest here, would you have the passion you do for these kids if you'd been reared in a more stable environment, where you didn't have to fight for everything you have?"

Hmm. She tried picturing a childhood the complete opposite of the one she'd lived. Nothing. The ever-changing environment she'd grown up in defined who she was today. All those unhappy experiences served as benchmarks to her for how to be a better advocate. She would be as demanding of herself in the roles of wife and mother if God blessed her with the chance for a family. That thought reminded her to stop hoping against hope for something not meant for her.

She had accomplished the first part of her dream—her job. She always kept the children and their needs as her focus when she was reviewing a file. She prayed every time she opened a case file, asking God to guide her in making the right decisions for the child whose well-being was in her hands.

The second half of her dream was a wavy blur. A mirage on the horizon that grew fainter the further down the path of life she journeyed. She didn't have time for anything else in her life. She had more than enough to keep her busy. And that's how she wanted it—needed it—to be.

"I'd have to think about that. But I don't have the luxury right now." Her gaze encompassed a large stack of file folders on her desk. "I believe the here and now is begging for my attention."

Gina never pushed her for all the details at one time on personal issues. Thank goodness she didn't pick now to change her pattern. Gina had no idea of the thoughts she'd stirred up with her question about an alternate childhood.

Gina smiled and handed her the folder. "Here is everything Nicky Boy has been doing since high school. It helps that he comes from an affluent family. Daddy works hard ensuring his name is in the paper on a regular basis. I still can't believe you don't read the society page. You would have already known most of this stuff if you did." Gina went back to her desk in the outer office and left Katherine to discover all Nick had achieved without the burden of an orphan's friendship to hold him back.

* * *

Nick's father swept into Nick's office on Thursday morning. "Good morning. Having a good week?"

Nick glanced up from the file he was reading. "Hi, Dad." And let out a long breath. "It's going."

This earned him a perplexed look. "Having problems with one of the kids?"

"No, the cases are fine. Judge Pierce wants me and the advocate to spend the weekend at his house in a team-building exercise."

His answer must have piqued his father's interest, because he moved from the doorway to a chair facing Nick and sat down. "Judge Pierce and I go way back. I've never considered him eccentric."

"Maybe family court requires thinking outside the box so the attorneys in his courtroom stay focused on the kids and how to work together."

"What aren't you telling me?" His father leaned forward, his jaw rigid, his gaze probing.

Nick rubbed a hand over his face, not looking forward to this conversation. "Nothing you need to worry about. Miss Harper and I didn't see eye to eye on something. Judge Pierce doesn't like tension in his courtroom, especially when a child is present. He thinks if we spend some time with him this weekend we'll all understand each other better and learn how to play together like good little boys and girls." At his father's raised eyebrow, Nick shrugged. "I'm just trying to keep my nose clean in his court."

"If you're uncomfortable with this, I can speak to Charles. Like I said, I've known him for a long time."

This didn't need fixing, at least not by his father. Couldn't he let Nick make his own mistakes so he could learn from them? "Thanks, Dad, but no. I'm out of my comfort zone and learning as I go." His lips quirked into a half-smile. "It'll all work out for the best."

"I don't want anything coming between you and that council seat."

"I won't do anything that tarnishes the Delaney name or ruins your big plans," Nick assured him.

His father nodded. "You'd better not, and don't get distracted by this children's advocate. You need to stay focused on achieving our goal."

Nick's jaw tightened, but he held his tongue. He'd learned how to pick his battles.

Chapter 4

On Friday afternoon, Nick pulled his SUV up in front of the two-story garage of a dark tan, cottage-style house. This was the address Gina, Katherine's assistant, had given his assistant. Cream-colored woodwork trimmed the front, and Katherine sat on a porch swing, her nose buried in a book. A small suitcase rested near the front steps. He took a fortifying breath and said a small prayer for guidance before he got out. This weekend was his best shot at cornering Katherine and finding out what she had against him.

"Hi. Thanks for letting me come by a few minutes early," he said and rested his foot on the bottom step.

Katherine closed her book with a snap and grabbed her oversized purse. "No problem since the judge insisted I ride with you."

He ignored her snarky tone and picked up the suitcase. Her position on the top step put them almost eye to eye. She had gold flecks mingled in the green of those expressive eyes. But he tethered his appreciation of her beauty and focused on the question that had been burning in his mind since the judge decreed they participate in this crazy weekend get-together. "You called Judge Pierce Uncle Charles when we were in chambers. Why?"

Her eyes went wide and she notched her chin in the air as if preparing for battle. She so didn't want to answer him. The gold flecks in her eyes glowed with that truth, but he wouldn't accept her silence. She owed him an answer.

The stiffening of her spine added an inch to her height, but he was still taller. He leaned closer to remind her of the fact. He'd stay right here all afternoon if he had to. Her eyes narrowed, and she may have growled. He wasn't sure. He smiled.

"Alice, the woman who adopted me, was a widow. Her late husband and Judge Pierce were first cousins. The judge handled the adoption, and since his and Aunt Melvia's son lives out of state, they sort of made me their surrogate niece."

Satisfied for now, he nodded and led the way to the back of his vehicle, where he stowed her case next to his black carry-on. Once he'd closed the gate, he turned and faced her. "I know this weekend's uncomfortable for you, but you have to know I never meant to hurt you, not back in high school, and not now either."

She didn't say anything, just swiveled on the ball of her foot like a ballerina and headed for the front passenger door. He rubbed a hand along the back of his neck. So much for extending an olive branch. Let her mope. He'd tried. After starting the car, he backed out of her driveway, as unsure of how they'd get along this weekend as he'd been when he arrived.

He stopped at a florist shop halfway to the judge's house. Before he got out, he asked if she wanted to come inside. She shook her head, pulled her book out of her bag and ignored him. In a few minutes, he was back and they were on their way.

They drove through tall, ornate wrought iron gates and followed the paved drive up to a two-story estate-style home in aged, brown brick. A lush lawn sprawled wide on either side and in front of the house. Semi-tamed woods surrounded the property and formed a natural privacy barrier. Nick stopped the vehicle even with the double glass-paneled doors of the house.

Judge Pierce came outside before Nick could pull their bags from the back of the vehicle. Two golden retrievers tugged against their leashes. "I see you made it."

Katherine abandoned her suitcase on the drive and knelt down. The judge freed the dogs. They lunged, almost knocking her over in their excitement. Nick rushed forward but wasn't fast enough. At her bubble of laughter, he relaxed as they nipped and danced around her, barking with excitement, vying for her attention.

"Buster. Bruno. Off, boys," she ordered in a stern voice. "I have your treats. Sit." She laughed when they dropped to their haunches and waited in quivering anticipation.

She rubbed their heads with affection before she reached into the oversized bag on her shoulder and pulled out two tufts of knotted rope, frayed at the ends. The dogs stayed seated but whined in recognition of the toys. She fished two doggie treats out of her bag and handed one to each of them before waving the ropes in front of them in temptation. They sprang to attention. She drew back and threw the ropes well past the drive, over into the cropped grass. Both dogs took off like arrows shot from a bow.

Katherine straightened and stepped into her uncle Charles's waiting arms. "There's my girl. Why don't you take the boys for their walk while I show Nick to his room?"

"That sounds great. I haven't played with them in forever." She hurried toward where the dogs played tug-of-war with one of the ropes.

Nick stood, enjoying her open display of affection while she played with the dogs. It was the first glimpse into a lighter, happier Katherine she'd allowed him to witness. He slung his bag over his shoulder and picked up her suitcase before nodding at the judge in greeting. "Sir."

"It's good of you to come willingly this weekend. It speaks well of you in my book."

He let the judge's comment go without a response and followed him up the stairs. Katherine's room was at the end of the hall on the left. Floral wallpaper resembling Victorian roses covered the walls. A lace-trimmed duvet on the bed in light cream offset the plush burgundy carpet muffling his footsteps. A make-up table and a Queen Anne chair sat against the wall opposite double doors that he guessed concealed a large closet.

After he set Katherine's case on the floor at the foot of the bed, the judge directed him across the hall to what would be his room for the weekend. Where Katherine's room was delicate and feminine, his was strong and masculine with an oversized chair in front of a gas fireplace and a large sleigh bed draped with a nautical-themed quilt. The carpet captured the turquoise color of the ocean. White walls provided a sharp contrast. A small writing desk with a deep walnut stain that matched the bed and wardrobe sat near a tall window, its wooden shutters open, letting in glimpses of the setting sun.

"I hope you'll be comfortable here," the judge said when Nick walked over to the bed and dropped his bag.

"It's fine. I would say thanks for having me, but since you didn't give me much choice, I don't think that's what you expect to hear."

He turned away from the intensity in the judge's eyes and prowled the room, exploring.

"I'm sure with Katherine's sense of fair play she's explained our family connection to you by now. That girl is special to me. She brought a dear friend an unlimited amount of joy when nothing else could after her husband died. I'll do anything I can to protect her."

The warning in his voice had Nick turning back to face him. "Don't forget, I knew Kat well before any of you did. I don't know why she's in denial over that fact, but I intend to find out this weekend."

"Be careful. Your father and I go back many years. I know how the Delaneys operate. You won't push and get your way here."

His jaw tightened at the judge's implication. "Exactly what are you saying? My father's a good man. He served as a children's advocate himself while I was in high school. I'm surprised he wasn't her appointed advocate for the short time she was in Pemberly."

The judge stood silent as if weighing his words. "I know about your father's time in family court. I won't form an opinion about you until I know you better. But be warned, I also know of your father's political aspirations for you. Don't even think about using situations in my courtroom to kick-start your political career."

Nick's muscles tensed, starting in his fists and climbing up his arms to the cords in his neck, and turning his jaw as rigid as granite. His nostrils flared. Judge or no judge, he wouldn't ignore the inferred slam against his character. "I assure you, I'm as aboveboard as any other man serving in your courtroom, regardless of my parentage."

Instead of continuing their unpleasant conversation, the judge suddenly changed the subject. "Dinner will be at seven. Katherine should be up soon. You can check with her and find out what help she'll need from you in the kitchen tonight." With that, he turned and left.

Nick let out a slow breath and looked upward. "Okay, God. What am I doing here? You have to show me, because I don't have a clue." Silence was his answer. He opened his bag and started unpacking. He was finished before he heard Katherine moving around next door.

He walked into the hall and tapped on her open door. She turned at the sound. He froze in mid-thought. Her antics with the dogs had left her cheeks flushed and her eyes shining with joy. She'd never looked more beautiful—more carefree.

"Judge Pierce said I should check with you for instructions." He stepped further into the room. "Nick Delaney reporting for duty, ma'am." He saluted. It was that or reach and smooth away the strand of hair clinging to her cheek. But she wouldn't welcome his touch.

With regret, he watched her smile slide into oblivion, replaced by the guarded look she wore when she dealt with him. "Give me five minutes and I'll meet you downstairs. The kitchen is at the bottom of the stairs, on the right." She turned back to her bag in dismissal.

Katherine entered the kitchen and found Nick rummaging in the refrigerator. She walked over and stood beside him.

He stepped back. "He bought plenty of vegetables. What do you plan to make?"

When she spotted carrots, onion, and broccoli in the crisper drawer, she knew what the judge wanted for dinner. She set the vegetables in the sink and put Nick to washing them. "We're having stir-fry with white rice. That okay with you?"

He raised his shoulders and let them drop in an exaggerated shrug. "Sure, what do you need me to do?"

After she explained how she wanted the vegetables sliced, she put a pot of water on to boil for the rice. She lined up the soy sauce and some other seasonings she knew the judge liked. They worked for several minutes in silence.

"What are you willing to share about yourself so I can contribute to our little 'show and tell' game at dinner?" His tone revealed his dislike of being at her mercy.

She measured seasoning into a cup, taking her time to answer. "I don't know yet."

"I have to share something about myself with you so it's not like it's a one-sided deal here, Katherine."

"I already know all I need to know about you." She met his mutinous glare with a satisfied smirk.

"How? We haven't said more than five words to each other before today and none of those were about me personally." He wiped his hands on a towel.

Her heart was beating double-time with the pleasure of revealing how she'd bested him. "I had Gina do some research for me. I know where you went to college, what your GPA was, and what you minored in. I know how long you've worked for Dear Ol' Dad, and when he made you a partner in the firm." She added the vegetables he'd chopped to the chicken she'd sliced and sautéed them in the pan with her back to him.

"So you're really going to hang me out to dry? That was your plan all along," he accused. He tossed the towel on the counter beside the stove. "Thanks. Thanks a lot."

She ignored the twinge of guilt his words stirred and met his glare over her shoulder. "I don't think of it as setting you up. I told you I didn't want to talk to you. I don't want to get to know you either. Nothing's changed."

She set the table while Nick called the judge to dinner. The judge said grace before they started. They passed the dishes around and filled their plates. But after a few minutes of fork to mouth, back to plate, it was evident neither she nor Nick planned to say anything.

Judge Pierce took the initiative. "So, who wants to go first?"

She looked up and smiled at Nick before she told the judge where he went to law school and what fraternity he'd joined.

Judge Pierce looked to Nick for confirmation. At Nick's nod, the judge smiled. "Good, now tell me, Nick, do you know where Katherine when to college?"

Katherine dropped her head and moved the food on her plate around in circles.

"We didn't get that far tonight. She spent all her time showing me what to do in the kitchen."

When she raised her head, she found his eyes trained on her. Was that a look of hurt on his face? He didn't have a reason to feel hurt. He'd betrayed *her*—tossed *her* out like yesterday's trash.

"That's no problem," the judge said. "I can fill you in on her schooling. She went to Stetson. She graduated summa cum laude with a double major in family law and child psychology, all while volunteering at several halfway houses and homeless shelters in the area. I tell you, this girl never stops." He slapped a hand on the table and Katherine jumped. "Alice worried she'd let herself get so run-down, she'd end up sick in the hospital. That's about the only way to make her slow down."

Her cheeks heated. Uncle Charles didn't have to get that personal in his recounting of her past. Nick, she noticed, was taking it all in.

"Katherine, dear, when we finish dinner, would you mind making some hot chocolate and joining me in my study for a cup?"

"I'd planned on doing the dishes right after we finished in here."

"Oh, don't worry about the dishes, Kat." Nick cut in, pouncing on a chance for payback. "You cooked. It's only fair I clean up. I may not be handy with a stove, but I'm pretty good with hot soapy water." He winked for good measure. The rat.

His response to her ungrateful glare was a smug smile when he took her plate and stacked it on top of his. She followed him into the kitchen but kept her back turned while she made the hot chocolate and he did the dishes. The atmosphere in the room was less than warm and she headed for the study faster than she wanted.

She carried the tray over to a table near Uncle Charles's old recliner. "I brought marshmallows."

"Your aunt Melvia won't let me have any. Since she's gone, I'll have three, please."

She smiled at the twinkle in his eye and added a fourth for good measure.

"Uncle Charles, I know what you're going to say. It wasn't fair when I didn't tell Nick anything about myself. But I'm not comfortable sharing things about myself with others, especially him. You don't know everything about my past."

"You have a lot of things going on in your life right now. You just lost your mother. Part of why I made you come here this weekend was so you'd rest. You've been burying yourself in your work. Use this weekend for what I intended. Give yourself time to remember Alice, to find peace and say goodbye to her."

He squeezed her hand. "She loved you so much. She was proud of all you've accomplished. But she wouldn't be happy knowing you're using those acts of charity to hide out from life, even the bad parts of it. You're no coward, so why are you doing it?"

"I experience the bad part of life every day. You see what we deal with in family court. I'm trying to keep as many children as I can from going through what I did. They need to know someone cares about them." She could justify everything she did. It was no one's business if she buried herself in her work as an escape from the loneliness that nipped at her heels, its bleakness waiting to claim her, swallow her up in its blackness.

"If you don't let yourself feel, even the hurt of losing someone you love, you can't heal. You won't be able to move on. You'll always be running from who you are, from what made you who you are."

He set his cup down. "Katherine, you mean the world to me. With Alice gone, you're stuck with me and my meddling ways. Give Nick a chance. He isn't the same boy you knew years ago any more than you're the same girl. Don't cheat yourself out of making a friend just because you're scared you'll get hurt again."

Her gaze clashed with his. "I don't want to be his friend. I don't want to be his anything. He'll finish his time in family court and be out of my life for good." She rose and kissed his cheek. "Thank you for caring enough about me to interfere, though."

The warmth of his concern and the cold weight of his request followed her out the door. He thought Nick had changed. That his respectful, responsible act was sincere. She knew better. He wanted the judge to back him for his candidacy. And the easiest way to win the judge's approval was befriending her.

Not this time. Nick Delaney's days of using her to get ahead were over.

Chapter 5

The next morning, a knock on her door woke Katherine from a sound sleep. When she peeked out into the hall, she found a breakfast tray on the floor with muffins, croissants, juice and coffee. She opened the door wider and looked across the hall. Nick's door stood wide open and he was nowhere in sight. She carried the tray inside and closed the door with her foot.

After her en suite breakfast and a quick shower, she went downstairs in search of the men. The kitchen was empty. She wandered around, searching the rest of the house. Nick was on the back porch with a mug of coffee and the morning paper, his feet propped up.

She stopped in the doorway, unsure he'd welcome her company. "Are you who I should thank for my breakfast?"

He glanced up and gave her a warm smile that darkened his eyes. "Yeah, I didn't want you to think you had to do everything. I pick breakfast up for the office on Fridays when I don't have court. I've gotten pretty good at to-go orders."

"Well, thanks. It was…it was nice of you." More than ready to move away from any further expressions of gratitude, she asked, "Where's Uncle Charles?"

"He took the dogs for a short walk through the neighborhood." Then he turned the conversation back to her. "I didn't know you liked dogs."

"A pet's one of the first things they told me I couldn't have when I went into foster care."

"Why don't you get one now?"

Typical Delaney logic. "I want" was good reason to do something, no matter how impractical. But she had responsibilities that kept her away from home into the evening. The desire for a pet was a little girl's dream. But she offered the practical excuse she used on herself whenever she walked past a pet store and willed herself to ignore the cute puppies in the window. "I'm never home. It wouldn't be fair to keep one crated all the time."

"I guess not."

She couldn't think of anything else to say. She rocked on her heels, her hands stuffed in her back pockets.

He rose and faced her. "Look, Kat. Excuse me, Katherine..."

"You can call me Kat outside the courtroom." Maybe that small concession would fool Uncle Charles into believing she was cooperating.

"Thanks. Why don't we trade information now? Then you won't have to talk to me again until after lunch."

He'd given her an out. She should be relieved. He must be as reluctant to be around her as she was to be around him. "Okay. What do you want to know about me?"

"What's your favorite color, your favorite time of day, and why?"

Huh? Of all the things he could ask, those shouldn't be on the list. She stared out over the lawn. "My favorite time of day is sunset. It relaxes me to watch the sun slip away. My favorite color is sapphire blue." She looked back and her gaze collided with eyes the exact shade she'd described. Her stomach lurched and she fought for breath.

He watched her for a long time without saying anything. The tightness built in her chest. She was an idiot. He wasn't the type of man to let an opening like that pass without some sort of smug comment.

"Now it's your turn."

She pasted on a false smile. "What do you do in your free time?"

"I play basketball on a community league team." He picked up his mug and the paper. "Thanks for sharing a little about yourself." He moved past her, leaving her alone on the porch.

She sat on the chaise longue, but got up after a few minutes and stood by the rail, staring out into the woods. Finally, she sat down in the chair he'd vacated. The scent of his spicy aftershave lingered on the cushion. She closed her eyes and breathed deep, not thinking about or wanting to feel anything.

Uncle Charles's weekend sabbatical was giving her too much time to think about herself and her life. She missed Alice. She drew a deep breath and released it slowly, settling the jumble of emotions this weekend had stirred within her. But she wasn't brave enough to go inside until she heard the dogs barking and knew Uncle Charles was back.

Nick was in the library when Judge Pierce and the dogs came in. "There you are," the judge said. "I'd hoped we'd get a chance to talk this morning." The dogs went over and lay down at Nick's feet.

At the judge's comment, he smiled sardonically. "Let me guess, you want to talk about Katherine."

"I do, but I also want to talk about you. What happened between you two in high school?"

Nick had tried to remember their history and his actions and couldn't think of a cause for Kat's animosity toward him now. But he knew in his bones that her behavior stemmed from some slight she blamed him for. He needed to figure out what that was and fix it. The judge was a good starting place.

"We had a math class and study hall together. She aced a big test I bombed. I asked her to tutor me and we became friends. At least, I thought we did.

"When my father found out my new study partner was a girl in foster care, he wasn't pleased. He ordered me to stay away from her. I promised him I would." He dropped his head, ashamed of his father's prejudices and his blind obedience. "He said I had to think about my future and my goals. If I ever wanted to hold a public office, I needed friends who were the right kind of people. He said if I didn't stop seeing her, he wouldn't pay for my tuition."

Judge Pierce listened without comment. "I see. And what did Katherine say to all this?"

Nick stared at him. "I couldn't tell her what my dad said. All I remember saying is that I had to start college early so I'd be too busy to hang out with her. That's the weird thing. I thought she took it pretty well. She said she understood and even wished me luck. By the next Monday, she had vanished. I called the group home. They told me she'd been transferred. Why would she do that only six weeks before graduation?" He got up and paced. He felt the same helpless frustration he'd experienced back then.

"I've thought about her a lot over the years. I wondered where she went, what she did with her life." He turned and smiled. "When I saw her in your courtroom I couldn't believe it. I never dreamed she was interested in law. She never mentioned anything about college or a career choice. It's obvious she's angry with me, but I don't know what I did."

"And Katherine requested the transfer?"

"When I asked him, my father said a lot of them feel like they have to move on. Maybe she was jealous of my chance to go away to school because she was stuck here." He rubbed his hands over his face in exasperation, not buying his words any more than he suspected the judge did. "I want to ask her, but when I try, she goes on the defensive and we end up snarling at each other."

The judge laughed. "At least you recognize what discussions between the two of you look like from where I'm sitting in the courtroom."

After a short silence, he offered Nick a hint of encouragement. "Maybe the two of you will learn how to talk by the end of this weekend."

Nick made no effort to hide his skepticism. "I hope you brought your gavel." He reached down and rubbed the dogs' ears.

"Give her time. And more importantly, let her know you care. She hasn't had very many people in her life who cared about her." The judge walked out, leaving him alone with the dogs.

A few minutes later Katherine came into the library and found Nick on the floor wrestling with Buster and Bruno. She turned to go.

"Wait."

She hesitated in the doorway. "Sorry, I thought Uncle Charles was in here."

Nick sat up and rested his back against the sofa. The dogs gave up on their play and stretched out in front of the hearth. "You just missed him."

He watched her. She tried not to squirm.

"Kat, can we talk? I mean, really talk."

One of her fears about this weekend was coming true.

She wanted to tell him so many things. At the same time, she didn't want to speak to him at all. She was stuck. If she walked out, she'd disappoint Uncle Charles and create more friction between her and Nick while they were in the courtroom. If she could just deal with him for the next month, he'd be gone from her life. This time, forever.

Resigned, she sat on the edge of the sofa with perfect posture and as far away from him as she could get. "Okay. What do you want to talk about?"

"What made you decide to practice law?"

"Alice, my adopted mother, helped me figure out what was important to me. She asked me what I would want if I could have anything. I said I wanted to be in charge, to have control over my life. I didn't like the way they did things in foster care, the way I was treated. She asked if I thought I could do a better job managing the lives of kids like me. I'd never thought of it that way. But I knew I could. I'd been where they were. I knew what they were going through, what scared them the most.

"She told me I had a lot to do if I wanted to go to law school. She introduced me to Judge Pierce and helped me sign up for scholarships. She and the judge had me do pre-law at community college and join the honors college before I applied to Stetson. She helped me find volunteer work that boosted my community resume." Katherine chuckled.

"She and Judge Pierce wrote recommendation letters and coached me on my interview. The college offered me a full ride on the spot. When I stood before the admissions board and they said I was exactly what they were looking for, it was surreal. I studied night and day, terrified I'd let Alice and Uncle Charles down. I cried when I received my diploma. Alice cried when I passed the bar. Judge Pierce helped me get my first job and had me assigned to his courtroom. He would never cop to it, but I think he cried after our first session."

Nick sat and listened as if he cared about her triumphs and struggles. He'd always been able to trick her into believing she mattered. To him. Then he smiled, like a shark flashing a mouth full of white teeth. "Maybe we should get started on lunch," he said and rose from the floor.

Katherine didn't know what Nick was up to, but he was up to something. He hadn't commented on her trip down memory lane after hounding her into talking to him. He'd just given her that toothy grin and jumped to his feet.

She got the ingredients for chicken salad out of the refrigerator and lined them up on the counter. He whistled while he worked. The sound was like nails on a chalkboard, and she wasn't having any luck tuning him out.

"Okay, what are you trying to do?" she asked after a few minutes of his off-key attempt at *The Andy Griffith Show* theme.

He had the gall to play dumb. "I don't know what you mean."

"You know exactly what I mean. You begged me to talk to you. I did, and you have no comment. There are no more questions about my past you need answered? I'm an attorney, too. We never let anything go."

"I understand that talking to me is more than you can handle right now. I don't want you to feel afraid or—" he paused, giving her a look that resembled pity "—inadequate. It's okay if you're uncomfortable sharing things about yourself with me."

She stood in stunned silence. If he thought for one minute that she was some wimpy crybaby who didn't know how to express the way she felt, then he was a complete idiot. "I am not afraid to talk to you about anything, Mr. Delaney!" She punctuated each word with a determined slice of her knife into the innocent onion at her mercy on the cutting board.

Nick had his back to her filling a pot with water. He made her wait until he finished his task and turned around. "I wouldn't want you to feel anxious."

"I'm not!"

"You're sure? I mean, if things get to be too much for you, just say the word." His concern bordered on patronizing. Her grip tightened on the knife and she fought the urge to choke him.

His worry and syrupy attitude were enough to make her gag. What was he up to? He couldn't think she was that weak. "Oh, for goodness sake, I survived foster care. I can answer any personal question you want to ask me."

"Okay. I'll take you at your word. Are you seeing anyone?"

"Excuse me?"

"I think that's a reasonable question. Your uncle mentioned you spend Friday nights with Jeremy. Is he your boyfriend? How serious are the two of you?"

"I don't have time for dating. I spend all my free time volunteering."

"So, who's Jeremy?"

"He's a friend from college. We do volunteer work together."

"Hmmm." He turned to set the timer for the eggs he'd put on to boil.

Katherine blew a wisp of hair out of her eyes and started dicing the chicken. "That's all you wanted to know? My dating status?"

"I was going to ask why you aren't married, but since you don't have time to date, there's the answer."

"I don't want to get married." She forced the words out between clenched teeth.

"Why not?"

There was no way she was explaining the whys of that statement to him. "I doubt it would work for me, so why bother?" She raised and dropped her shoulders in a dismissive move. "Men in political office tend to be married. What about you?"

"What about me?"

"Are you seeing anyone?"

"No one serious. I stay busy with work, too. But unlike you, I'm not opposed to marriage. I have an image of the right woman for me. I haven't found her yet."

Her hands stilled. "An image?"

Nick opened the fridge and got the mayonnaise. "Not a physical image. A personality. I want someone who shares the same concerns for the community. Someone willing to go with me to political and corporate dinners because she likes being with me, even if she hates the social hobnobbing."

"Oh, I get it. You want a trophy wife. Arm candy."

His answer was immediate and defensive. "I won't marry to advance my career." He ignored her snort of disbelief. "I want someone who knows the real me. Who can sense from across the room that I need rescuing. A partner I can discuss problems with, who will offer intelligent, insightful suggestions on how to fix those problems."

"Sorry, I don't know any social butterflies with political goals. I don't attend many dinner parties."

"Why is that?"

She organized their lunch on a tray while he put ice in the glasses for tea. "I don't have time. Family court doesn't require hobnobbing. Besides, *I* don't have any political aspirations."

Nick released the dogs from their leashes once they reached the woods. The dogs took off, barking and chasing squirrels. He and Katherine jogged to keep up but were no match for the dogs' exuberance. They found a place to rest against a fallen tree.

He watched Katherine as she ran her fingers over the rough bark of the tree trunk. "Are you really serious about never getting married?"

She glanced up. "I think marriage should involve love, but I…" Her voice trailed off.

"You what?"

"Nothing." She slid from the log and walked farther down the path toward where the dogs circled a tree, eyeing a squirrel out of their reach.

He went after her. "There's no *nothing* now. What were you going to say? Come on, Kat—you said you could handle the questions."

With her back to him, she balled her fists at her sides and took a deep breath before she faced him. Her eyes were vacant, cold. "My mother loved my father, too much. And then I let myself care about someone. But he wasn't who I thought he was. He did help me realize the level of emotions involved in our relationship were very uneven. I thank God every day I found out before I did something too stupid to take back. So, you see, I'm not a good long-term risk. I can't commit because I'm not capable of loving a man the way you should for a relationship to work. I would never trust that he loved me that much."

The hurt in her eyes matched the quiver of emotion in her voice. But he knew she showed her capacity to love every day. She poured her heart, her soul, into those kids she helped, one case at a time.

"Is that why you dump all your love into your work?" He kept his voice quiet, almost gentle. Her answer was important. Somehow, he believed the world would be dimmer if she gave up hope.

She looked at him in bewilderment. "My work? What has my job got to do with love?"

"Uh, you think what you do doesn't require love?"

"No, what I do involves compassion. There isn't room for love in my job. I deal with abandoned, neglected children who have tender emotions. I'm a temporary fixture in their lives. I can't let them get too attached to me or they'll be hurt even worse when they get transferred." Her voice was raw, edged with the emotions she fought to control, but they flickered across her face, reflecting in her expressive eyes.

"No, reading their case files and making a recommendation for their care is your job. Driving a little boy to see his grandmother on weekends goes beyond an act of compassion." He stepped away, then turned back. "I get that you want to keep your heart safe. You only share your emotions with the revolving door of cases you handle because you think it will stop you from getting hurt."

He drew in a deep breath, while she stood motionless. "But there will come a day when a guy takes one look at you and that big marshmallow of a heart you have and he'll recognize what a treasure you are. He won't be able to let you go." He walked up to her and cupped her cheek in his hand, his words a whispered plea. "When he does, at least give him the chance to love you as much as you deserve." He dropped his hand and moved toward the dogs.

"I can assure you, no man is going to walk into court and decide I'm his dream come true. I live in the real world. I'm happy being alone. My life is full. You're the one looking for a partner, not me."

The anger and bitterness in her words caught him by surprise and he called her bluff. "You're right. I'm the one who doesn't want to spend the rest of my life coming home to an empty apartment. I want someone who's not afraid to share my dreams, my love. You're hiding from the real world. So keep on volunteering and avoid living life and stay safe. No one will ever be able to touch that precious heart of yours."

Her chest was heaving. She flung each word at him like a rock meant to do him harm. "I'm not hiding from anything. Do you know how many kids I help doing what I do? How many battered women I give free legal advice? I am living. I don't need a man to tell me I'm worth something. My worth shows in the people I help. The lives I change for the better."

Buster and Bruno reacted to her distress. They whined and pawed at her for attention. She reached down and rubbed their backs until they quieted.

He didn't want to fight with her. He cared about her. But it wasn't in his power to make her happy. He asked God to give her peace, to comfort her. To show her there was someone out there for her. That she wasn't meant to be alone.

"I'm sorry." His voice gentled. "But I think you sell yourself short. You're worth far more than the job you do, as great as you are at it. Has anyone ever nominated you for Citizen of the Year?"

She growled and looked like she was going to scratch his eyes out.

"What? I'm serious. You do so much to help the people of this community. That's what the award is for, isn't it?"

"What is it with that stupid award?" She threw her hands up and stalked back toward the house.

He jogged to catch up with her. "What'd I say?"

Once they reached the house, Nick hurried to clean up before coming into the kitchen, ready to help and talk to her some more. Now that she was finally opening up, he wasn't giving her a chance to slide back into her shell.

"What are we making?"

"*I'm* making a strawberry pizza."

"Strawberry pizza? You mean strawberries with tomato sauce?"

She laughed. "Think of it as a big cheesecake with a strawberry glaze."

"O-kaayyyy, that's better. But I still don't know where the pizza comes in. But you're the boss. What do you need me to do?"

"I need four cups of sliced berries."

They worked in companionable silence. He split his attention between slicing berries and watching her make the glaze. But when she opened the fridge and set the pot from the stove on one of the shelves, his curiosity won out. "What are you doing? That's a hot pot you put in there."

"I know. I put a trivet on the shelf. Trust me, it'll be fine."

"If you say so.

She shook her head and offered him a rueful smile. "It's the judge's favorite. Alice always made this for him on his birthday."

"I'll wait until I've taste it before passing judgment." After a long pause, he continued his questions. "Where did you learn to cook?"

She was stirring graham cracker crumbs and melted butter together in a bowl. She stayed silent so long, he wasn't sure she'd answer. "I volunteered for kitchen duty at the group homes where I stayed. The bullies wouldn't be caught dead doing KP so it was a safe place. The cooks always appreciated an extra pair of hands, no matter how inept. Eventually they shared techniques and recipes." She dumped the mixture into a glass dish and smoothed it out with a spatula before popping it into the oven.

She carried the bowl she'd used to mix the ingredients over to the sink, turned on the faucet, and grabbed the soapy sponge. "The hardest thing after I was out of foster care was remembering to reduce the recipes. I was used to feeding twenty people."

Nick took the bowl from the drying rack and wiped it with a towel. "Well, we always had a cook. Unless she left milk and cookies on the table, the kitchen was off limits. I learned how to microwave frozen dinners and boil water while away at college, but that's as good I can do."

They stood next to each other, working in tandem. She washed and rinsed. He dried and stacked. When she handed him the last dish, she said, "Maybe you should add cooking to your list of requirements for that partner you're after. She's sounding more and more like a hostess. I hear Abby Blackmon's available. Tell her you're nice to small children and you'll score some extra brownie points."

He clenched his jaw, but held his tongue.

"Dinner's almost ready. Nick, I was teasing." The ding of the oven timer distracted her.

He left while her back was turned.

Their meal consisted of a beef roast she'd cooked in the crockpot with vegetables. Dinner conversation, however, was subdued and stilted. The judge pounced on their lack of communication. "Anything happen while you were out with the dogs?"

"No, we were fine." She shifted the carrots around on her plate. "Nick thinks someone should nominate me for Citizen of the Year."

The judge choked on his food. Nick leaned back out of the line of fire.

"Well, you should be nominated." The judge pounded his fist on the table like a gavel.

"I completed that volunteer history because of emotional blackmail. I'm still not happy with you."

The judge ignored her and turned toward Nick. "I have friends on the committee that selects the Citizen of the

Year. This year they've asked me to speak. I thought it would be a good idea to have Katherine and other volunteers document the work they do so the committee can see how many charities benefit from the volunteers' hard work within our community."

"I think Abby Blackmon is the ideal nominee," she said. "Her father donated a truckload of money to build that new children's wing. She speaks well. She photographs well. She's used to being in the limelight and attends charity luncheons. People doing the grunt work belong in the background."

Uncle Charles nailed her with a stern glare. "Well this time you will be front and center, young lady. I have a table reserved with your name on one of the place cards. It starts at six Friday night. You'd better not be late." With a smile, he motioned to Nick. "Would you care to join us?"

Nick took the opportunity to score a point of his own. "My father wanted me to call and see if Abby Blackmon was available."

Kat's glance jumped to his. He smiled. "I told him I could arrange my own dates. I'll be happy to go and I won't need a date. I'll bring Kat, to make sure she arrives on time," he promised, without taking his eyes off her. "You don't mind riding with me, do you?"

"Don't put yourself out on my account. I'm more than able to drive myself."

He leaned forward. "That's okay. I don't mind. Besides, it'll free up a parking space." His eyes twinkled with laughter in answer to her glare.

The judge missed the undercurrent, or maybe not, because he gave his hearty approval. "That's an excellent idea. Katherine, you'll ride with Nick."

"Fine. Who wants dessert?" She rose from the table,

tossed her napkin over her plate and stalked toward the kitchen.

She returned with a dish of fluffy white filling topped with a bright red sauce loaded with berries and set it in the middle of the table. "There's some spaghetti sauce in the kitchen. I could drizzle some over your piece." She threw him an impish smile.

"Don't you dare. I'll take a serving just like it is."

"It might taste terrible."

"No. Sometimes a man knows with one look when some-thing's perfect." His gaze locked with hers.

Her hand wobbled when she handed him a plate loaded with a generous serving. With his first bite, his eyes slid closed and he moaned in pleasure.

"If you're this crazy about food, you need to either take cooking lessons or marry a chef."

"Why are you so ready to push me down the aisle?"

"You said you were looking for a partner. I'm trying to help you in your search."

Chapter 6

On Sunday morning, Katherine followed the judge and Nick through the atrium and into the sanctuary of Grace Community Church. The judge claimed the aisle seat and waited for Nick and her to settle into their seats. She scooted down until there was enough room for two people to sit between her and Nick.

The judge leaned forward with a frown. He cleared his throat and motioned for her with a crook of his finger. "Katherine, dear, I forgot my bulletin. Would you mind getting me one?"

What could she say? They were in church. Never mind that the old fox was trying to outmaneuver her. She stood and slid past Nick and him as she exited the pew. When she came back with the requested bulletin, an older couple had taken her spot. The only available space was between Nick and the judge.

As she slid back into the pew, the toe of her shoe tapped the judge's shin. He grunted and looked up. When their eyes met, his twinkled. She mumbled what wouldn't pass for an apology if he heard it.

She sat through the service caught between Nick and the judge as if they were bookends holding her in place. The judge shifted, forcing her to readjust her position closer to Nick. Her muscles screamed from holding herself rigid throughout the service. She didn't want to chance prolonged contact with Nick. To block out the scent of his woodsy aftershave, she focused on Pastor Jeremy Walker's sermon.

He reminded them of God's love and the importance of men forgiving their brothers, the way Christ forgave us, and tossed our past sins into the sea of forgetfulness.

Her spirit always felt lighter after one of Jeremy's sermons. But today, his words weighed heavy on her heart. It wasn't easy to forgive and forget. She knew that. She hadn't considered forgiving Nick and his father. She just wanted to forget them.

Nick shifted in his seat, reminding her of his presence and the brutal reality that she couldn't run from her past. She had to face it, and him, before she could move on. She closed her eyes and prayed for God's guidance in how to do that.

After the service, Jeremy stood at the main entrance. Katherine and the judge moved forward, but Nick lagged behind.

The judge pumped Jeremy's outstretched hand in a firm handshake. "I enjoyed your sermon. It's good to remind us how important it is to forget the past so we're free to embrace the future."

Jeremy looked at Katherine. The smile on his face reached his eyes when he embraced her. "Katherine, I thought since you couldn't make it Friday night I wouldn't be seeing you this morning."

"I told you I'd be with Uncle Charles."

"Oh, Jeremy, let me introduce Nick Delaney." The judge motioned Nick forward. "He's serving in my court with Katherine for the next month."

Jeremy extended his hand in a neutral greeting.

"Pastor." Nick's response was as cool.

Katherine wondered at Jeremy's uncharacteristic stiffness. But then, Nick appeared standoffish too. There was no time to dwell on their odd behavior. They were holding up the line of members scrambling for Jeremy's attention. Jeremy squeezed her hand before Nick grasped her elbow and guided her away.

Back on the road, Nick cut his eyes to the rearview mirror and watched Katherine.

"He's your Friday night date?"

A blush stole across her face. "He's a friend."

He waited for her to elaborate, but she held silent. "Judge Pierce, are we free to go once we get back to your house?"

"You two have fulfilled my requirements. I trust you will remember this experience and behave with more civility in my courtroom in the future."

"Absolutely. Yes, sir." They answered at the same time.

After they dropped the judge at home, Nick stowed both of their bags in his vehicle. He shook hands with the judge, promising to deliver Katherine on time to the awards dinner.

They drove off in silence. He tugged his tie loose then merged with the traffic. "I guess this is two Friday nights you'll miss seeing Jeremy."

"He'll be at the ceremony." She rotated as much as her seat belt would allow. "In fact, I can ride with him so you don't have to go out of your way."

Was that desperation in her voice? He glanced over, but she'd turned away. At a red light, he laid his hand over hers. She jumped and his lips quirked into a half smile. "I don't mind. Besides, if you don't show, the judge will blame me."

She glared. For the rest of the drive, he left her to her own thoughts. He set her overnight bag on the porch at her house and waited until she'd unlocked the front door. "I'll see you Tuesday morning in court, Miss Harper. Have a good night."

"Thanks. You too."

As he backed out of Katherine's driveway, Nick pulled his cell phone out and punched speed dial. His basketball buddy answered on the second ring.

"I thought you might call," Jeremy said, his voice tinged with laughter.

"Funny, very funny. Are you home or did you take some single parishioner out to lunch?"

"Actually, I went to lunch with Senator and Abby Blackmon. She's very beautiful." Jeremy sighed.

"I've heard that. Are you at home? We need to talk." He didn't bother disguising the edge in his voice.

"Ah, so the new attorney who's driving Katherine Harper crazy is you. I had no idea you two knew each other that well."

"We haven't seen each other in a long time." Nick pulled over on the side of the road for safety. "It's complicated. Can I come over or not?"

"There's no service tonight so I'm free for the afternoon. We can watch the game while we talk."

Not twenty minutes later, Nick pulled up in front of the ranch-style parsonage Pastor Jeremy Walker called home. Before he could ring the doorbell, Jeremy opened the door.

"Come on in." Jeremy stepped back and threw his arm out in an open gesture. As soon as Nick stepped inside, Jeremy nailed him with the question he'd expected. "Tell me why you didn't want Katherine and Judge Pierce to know we're friends."

Nick followed him into the den, where a flat-screen TV was mounted on the wall. He sat down in the twin to the leather recliner Jeremy called his "quarterback-coaching" chair. "I didn't know you were the Jeremy she volunteers with on Friday nights. I finally have her where she'll open up to me and I thought if she knew about our connection, she'd clam up again."

Jeremy folded his arms across his chest. "Uh-huh. That makes so much sense."

"What did you mean when you said I was the attorney making Kat's life crazy?"

"Oh, no, you don't." Jeremy wagged a finger at him. "I will not betray one friend to another."

"It's not a betrayal." Nick was on his feet, moving to stand by the bookshelf. He fingered the neat rows of books. "I want to learn more about her and it's a constant battle." He looked back at his friend.

"Maybe you should start at the beginning."

"When did y'all meet?" Nick said, not happy with the obvious concern Jeremy was expressing over Kat.

"That meant *you* were supposed to start at the beginning, not me."

"I will, but I want to know how far back you two go before I fill in any gaps."

"Katherine and I met in junior college in Psychology 101. I was dabbling in a lot of volunteer work. Mrs. Harper had just adopted her. She and Judge Pierce had her volunteering a lot so Katherine could improve her chances of acceptance into law school. She and I volunteered at Grace Community. Her friendship and encouragement are the main reasons I stayed. I've never seen someone with so much love to give." Jeremy finished his story with a fond smile on his face.

"Well, don't get any ideas about her giving you that love," Nick warned.

Jeremy quirked an eyebrow. "Excuse me? I thought you two were at war?"

"I'm working on that."

"The war or the peace treaty? Maybe you should tell me how *you* met Katherine."

"We went to high school together. My dad handled some advocacy cases. He found out my new best friend was a kid in foster care and flipped out. He demanded I stop seeing her. When I told her I was starting college a semester early, she bailed. I never saw her again. I called her the next week. They said she requested a transfer." Nick rubbed the back of his neck. "She didn't even tell me goodbye."

"I don't think she does goodbyes very well," Jeremy offered. "She's heard too many of them. I was so worried about her at Alice's funeral. Everyone she's loved has left her. But she seemed better today, even after a weekend spent with your ugly mug."

He ignored Jeremy's slam. "When did she die?"

"Alice? About a month ago. I did the service. Katherine stood there all alone, looking so lost. Even Judge Pierce couldn't get her to go home with him and his wife. She came by my office last week, more upset than I've seen her in a long time. The judge was pushing her for the volunteer paperwork and some guy from her past wanted to be her best friend. She made it sound like he was harassing her. You wouldn't possibly have become obsessive in your attempts to get her to talk to you, would you?"

"I didn't know she was facing all that." Nick threw his hands up, guilt over the added pressure he'd put on her heavy on his conscience. "My first day in court, the judge suggested a postponement, but she refused. I had no idea she'd lost her mom." He rubbed his hands over his face. "I thought it was the shock of seeing me. Ahhhhh. I must have been the last person she needed to face right then. No wonder she freaked when I kept trying to talk to her."

"Yeah, well, not all the ladies think you're Mr. Wonderful. When I met Katherine, she made it clear she didn't want anything beyond friendship. She said she would never be stupid enough to care about a guy again. Want to tell me what you did to her?" Jeremy hit him with an accusing glare.

"Me? Why do you assume it was me?"

"Let's see, it was our freshman year in college and I know how busy she was the last few weeks before graduation so the last guy she admits to coming in contact with was...you."

"I don't know what I did or said that made her feel that way. Maybe it was the fact I was going away to school and she had to stay behind."

"I don't think so. This smacks of something personal. Were you two dating?"

"I wish, but no."

His response earned him another raised eyebrow. "Care to elaborate on that?"

"I was going to ask her out. But before I could, my dad ordered a 'cease and desist'. I never got the chance. She was very shy. It took me weeks to get her to agree to tutor me in math, and she knew how bad I'd bombed our last exam. The whole class knew."

"I don't know if you want some friendly or godly advice, but I'm going to give you both. Pray—a lot—and then talk to her. Ask her if you did something to hurt her. If she's willing to tell you, then ask her to forgive you. Then your conscience is clear and she'll see you're sorry you hurt her and maybe her heart can heal."

"You assume I hurt her." He glared at Jeremy. "I cared about her. I wouldn't have done anything to hurt her."

"Maybe it's an imagined slight that grew over time." Jeremy walked over to him. "All I can tell you is the young woman I met in college bore some deep emotional wounds.

I wanted to go out with her, but God helped me see she needed a friend more than she needed a boyfriend. I've never regretted my choice. And even though I'm your friend, if you hurt her, I'll do more than skunk you on the basketball court. I mean it, Nick. You be gentle with her."

Nick listened in astonished silence as his friend and teammate threatened him with bodily harm. Jeremy was a man of God. Yet he'd all but said he'd take Nick out behind the woodshed if he even thought about hurting Kat.

"You're sounding a little too protective for a guy who claims he's only her friend."

"Yeah, well, if she'd given me a chance to be more, I'd have taken it. She's something special and the guy she gives her heart to will have it forever."

"You're right, he will." Nick let out a deep sigh. "I'll talk to her. But I'll give her time to recover from putting up with me all weekend before I try." He turned to leave. "Thanks for caring enough about her and me to be honest with me. I can see how much she means to you. She means a lot to me, too. I would never do anything to intentionally hurt her." He shook Jeremy's hand at the door.

Nick drove home, his mind busy examining every word and gesture from the past weekend. He mixed in all the facts Jeremy had shared with him about their college days and fought against the green-eyed monster over the time he'd been away, in another state, trying to forget her—the girl who'd left him. He was in awe of the woman she'd become, and disheartened that she couldn't stand to be in the same room with him.

Sunday evening, Katherine's nerves wouldn't settle enough to allow her to work on the case files she'd brought home. Jeremy's sermon and Nick's repeated claims that he cared for her made her uneasy. Jeremy had said you had to forgive your brother for the pain his actions caused you, or the hurt would keep you from drawing closer to God.

That wasn't fair! She was the one they lied to, the one they threw away like trash. Why did she have to be the one to forgive when they weren't sorry for what they did? She didn't want anything to keep her from having a closer relationship with God, but she sure didn't feel ready to forgive. She gave up on work and stuffed the paperwork back into her briefcase, turned out the lights and went to bed.

Snuggled under the covers, in her own house, far away from Nick Delaney, her body and mind relaxed, and she fell asleep. But one night of sound sleep didn't make up for a weekend spent on constant guard against Nick's attempts to charm her. She awoke almost as tired as she'd been when she'd gone to bed.

Fortified with two cups of coffee, she arrived at work to find Gina too perky for a Monday morning. "What's got you already buzzing like a bumblebee this morning?" Katherine asked after she walked in on Gina humming along with the radio playing through the speaker system.

"It's not me—it should be you." She pointed toward Katherine's office.

Katherine glanced back as she headed toward her door to see if Gina would say any more. At Gina's unusual silence, she stepped inside with trepidation. Smack dab in the middle of her desk sat the most exotic orchid with satin petals in lavender and pink.

"Oh." Her awe over receiving such a delicate and beautiful flower impaired her tongue.

"Oh? You're kidding, right? Like you don't know who sent it," Gina accused. At her blank look, Gina ordered, "Hurry up and read the card before I die of curiosity."

"How did you keep from doing that already?" Katherine teased as she set her briefcase in a chair and reached with nervous fingers for the white envelope with her name stenciled in black.

> *Thanks for putting up with me. I thought about cut flowers, but they fade. I wanted you to have something that would last. Nick.*

She worried her lip and ran a finger along one of the satiny petals.

Gina hovered at her shoulder. "Well?"

"It's from Nick." Katherine tucked the card in her pocket, knowing Gina wouldn't let an opportunity to snoop go by if she left it out.

"I guess that means the weekend went better than you thought it would."

His gift, and the note attached, tugged at something deep inside her, but Katherine forced it back and held tight to the hurt and pain from her past. She used them to remind herself she couldn't trust him. Flowers and sweet words were easy, and Nick Delaney had all the moves of a charmer down pat. He wanted to make a good impression on the judge. And maybe he even wanted to soften her up.

"It was fine." She moved the flower to her credenza and checked the soil's dampness. "You and I need to go shopping today."

"You don't shop," Gina reminded her. "You think lunchtime trips to the mall are for debutantes, not us regular working girls." Gina quoted Katherine's favorite excuse when invited along for a lunchtime visit to the world of foofooism.

"If I'm expected to go to the awards dinner and listen to Uncle Charles' speech, I need a new dress. Especially since Nick will be at our table."

"You're his date?" Gina's mouth curved into an appreciative feline grin.

"Stop drooling. No, I'm *not* his date. He maneuvered it so I have to ride with him. His father wanted him to take Abby Blackmon but if he takes me he won't have to get a real date."

"He said that? To your face?" When Katherine nodded, she added, "He is a jerk."

"Yep, he did and he is." She rested her hands on her hips and notched her chin. "So we're going shopping and I'm buying the most debutante-worthy gown I can find."

Gina's eyes took on a wicked sparkle. "Are you going to let me do your hair? You know I love playing dress-up." She reached out and unclipped Katherine's thick mane of hair, twisting and twirling it around her fingers. "There are so many things I can do with all this." She held a handful in front of Katherine's face.

"Sure. I don't have court Friday. We'll take a half day."

"Great. Lunch today is my treat. Right after we find you the perfect dress."

Shopping wasn't bad. She just had better things to do with her limited free time than indulge in such extravagance. Only a good cause could force her to participate in the ritual. Uncle Charles giving a speech at an awards dinner fell under the "good cause" category. The chance to pop Nick Delaney's eyes out was a bonus. But that was selfish. And petty. Katherine smirked. She was human after all.

She and Gina found the perfect dress at the first store they visited. Both of them were smiling when they got back to the office, Katherine with a new floor-length gown and all the accessories, per Gina's insistence, and Gina with new shoes and matching handbag to go with a dress she'd already purchased.

Katherine took her dress home at the end of the day and hung it on her closet door, where it would stay until Friday night. The shiny fabric caught her eye each time she came out of the bathroom. She tried to ignore both the dress and the tiny knot of tension winding tighter each day as Friday crept closer.

The dress was beautiful. There was no doubt about that. But the thought of stepping out of her comfort zone just to prove to Nick she was as good as him—and possibly failing because she had no idea what she was doing—upped her anxiety several notches.

Alice's advice would've been to stand tall and look him in the eye. She could do this. She equated her preparations for the evening with the Bible's command to gird your loins before a battle. She let out a determined breath and prayed for victory.

She'd missed her senior prom thanks to Edward Delaney's arranged transfer, though she would have spent the night holding up a wall like all the other outcasts. Foster kids were not members of the popular cliques. But if she'd gone to a dance back then, she'd know what to expect now. A girlie girl she was not.

There hadn't been any classes on prepping for a big social event in law school, which put her at Gina's mercy. A scary prospect in and of itself. Gina's imagination was way too vivid for Katherine's peace of mind. Gina had cast herself as the fairy godmother and wanted Katherine and Nick to play Cinderella and Prince Charming.

With a tired sigh, she dismissed her apprehensions. Tomorrow night would be nothing more than an elegant dinner spent with Uncle Charles, Aunt Melvia, Jeremy, Gina and, she sighed again, Nick. She would only be alone with him for the short drive to the hotel and back. The rest of the time, she'd be with friends. She could do this. *God, please help me.*

This wasn't a date. Nick had said so himself. This was an attempt to use her to look good in front of Uncle Charles.

That reality snapped in two the ball of tension building in her stomach. In its place was the familiar burn of determination. She'd show him what he'd thrown away and smile when she stepped over him after he fell at her feet begging for forgiveness.

The next afternoon Katherine soaked in a tub filled with lavender scented water with cool slices of cucumber resting over her eyes. She buffed and pampered herself more than she ever had in her life, and it was all Gina's fault.

She'd convinced Katherine she needed to experience the whole effect to get into the debutante act properly. "It will relax you. Put you in the right frame of mind to be around Nick for several hours while he's in his element. It's a means of leveling the playing field," Gina had argued. And Katherine was so gullible she fell for it.

Gina arrived armed with what looked like a mobile salon. She draped Katherine in a smock and got busy. She misted, twisted, curled and pinned until she'd achieved her vision. Finally, she handed Katherine a mirror so she could see for herself.

The look of surprise and the sound of awe that escaped her newly plum-tinted lips were Gina's payment.

"I told you," Gina boasted.

"Wow. You've made me look...I don't know how to describe it. Beautiful is too tame a word for this." Katherine turned her head from one side to the other, using the hand mirror to get a better view. When her eyes met Gina's, she fought the sting of tears. "I don't know how to thank you for doing all this."

Gina tweaked a hairpin. "Be sure and tell me what Nicky Boy's reaction is when you open the door. That will be reward enough."

Half an hour after Gina left, Katherine was coming down the stairs when she heard a car door close. The doorbell chimed at the same time her cell phone rang. With her head down, rummaging for the phone in her evening bag, she opened the front door.

"Hello," she said by way of greeting to both the caller and her visitor.

"Uncle Charles, yes, he's at the door." Katherine smiled and handed the phone to Nick.

He didn't move. She wasn't sure he was breathing. His gaze was stuck to her. She held the phone to his ear where the judge's voice boomed. The sound brought him back to reality and he clasped the phone with his hand.

"Yes, sir, we're ready." His smile could have lit up half of Pemberly, "She's beyond stunning."

Katherine's stomach fluttered.

"We're on our way." He clicked the phone off and handed it back to her. "Wow. You look gorgeous." He beamed another mega-watt smile. His eyes roamed over her, taking in the eggplant-colored evening gown. He took her hand and turned her in a circle. "Absolutely stunning."

His compliment had her heart thudding in her chest. But she wouldn't let his words sway her. She reminded herself he had an agenda. She was a means to an end for him, nothing more. It wouldn't pay to get all dreamy-eyed now.

"Thanks. We should go or we'll be late."

He offered his arm and led her out to his car. He opened her door and waited until she positioned the long skirt of her dress around her legs. He'd left the SUV at home in favor of a dark BMW sedan. Neither one spoke on the short drive to the hotel as Nick maneuvered through the heavy downtown traffic. She focused on hiding her nervousness, struggling not to fidget whenever he glanced her way.

An usher at the door directed them to their table. Abby Blackmon was sitting next to Jeremy. He stood and greeted

Katherine when they walked up. "Katherine, you look beautiful." He gave her a casual hug. "Have you met Abby?"

Katherine smiled and said thanks before turning to Abby. "Yes, Abby and I have worked on several charity boards together. How are you doing tonight?"

"I'm well. It's great to see you again, Katherine. I love your dress."

Gina arrived, followed by Judge Pierce and Aunt Melvia, along with members of the selection committee. Dinner included grilled chicken served with seared pineapple, rice, and asparagus, along with garden salad and dinner rolls. Close to time for dessert, the committee members and the judge excused themselves to take their places on the raised dais.

"On behalf of the selection committee I would like to thank all of you for attending tonight's Citizen of the Year awards dinner. I'm Judge Charles Pierce and it's my honor to present this year's award. The recipient has lived in this and some of our neighboring communities all her life. But she never received the advantages some of us took for granted while growing up. She didn't have a stable home environment, and in fact, found herself entrusted to state care before she turned ten."

When he began his speech, Katherine had stopped eating, granting him her undivided attention, knowing how excited he was about presenting the award tonight. But when his speech touched on the recipient's tragic upbringing, a hot pressure gripped her chest. The air squeezed from her lungs. She threw a panicked glance over to Aunt Melvia. She was smiling back at her while tears slid down her cheeks.

And that's when she knew. He was talking about her. Revealing the pathetic story of her life for the whole town to hear. She wanted to run, but made herself concentrate on taking slow, even breaths. She didn't look around. Too afraid she'd see the looks of pity on their faces as the judge trotted her life out for inspection. She forced herself to listen to the rest of the speech, trying to detach herself from the story. *Pretend it's one of your cases.*

"This year's recipient didn't take the disadvantages she faced as anything but a challenge, a chance to prove the system wrong. She maintained excellent grades in school. In her senior year of high school, she met a woman who became her mentor. Who challenged her to be anything she wanted, who convinced her hard work would take her wherever she wanted to go."

She tried not to squirm while he listed all the charities and other community causes she volunteered with.

Nick leaned over and whispered in her ear. "You realize he's talking about you?"

She nodded but kept her head down. As Uncle Charles wound down from his long list of her accomplishments, a new dread filled her. They'd want her to walk up there and accept the award. To thank them for their pity. They expected her to say something. Her mind was blank. She had no idea what to say to all these people. Why had she given in and filled out that stupid form?

"The reason they let me have the honor of presenting the award this year is because the young lady I've been describing is a family member of mine, so to speak. My cousin by marriage, Alice Harper, adopted Katherine Jenkins right before she turned eighteen. Katherine is a children's advocate serving in family court under my jurisdiction. She's more than an attorney, more than a friend to this community. She's more than a children's advocate. She is a true advocate of love for all people, willing to help anyone in any way she can. So, without any further bragging from me, may I present Pemberly's Citizen of the Year, Miss

Katherine Harper." He stepped back, applauding. As his eyes met hers, he smiled his pride at all she'd accomplished.

The heat of a blush rushed across her cheeks. Unsure what to do, she looked around the table. Jeremy and Nick stood and escorted her to the stage. Jeremy kissed her on the cheek and Nick kissed her hand before leaving her at the steps to the dais.

Uncle Charles wrapped her in his arms, giving her a crushing hug. In a soft voice meant for her ears alone, he said, "I'm so proud of you. I promised Alice I'd do this, but I wanted to even before she asked me. We are so blessed to have you in our family."

Katherine fought against the emotions welling up, refusing to cry over the judge's private words in front of these strangers. She accepted the plaque and looked out over the room full of guests. They had risen in her honor and were still clapping.

"Thank you very much, Uncle Charles." She offered him a watery smile. "And thank you to the members of the selection committee. I know there are numerous people who have done so much more than I have. I think we should honor them, as well. The things I do, the people I help, I don't do for an award, or even a thank-you. I do it because I see a need." Her voice took on an impassioned earnestness. "And if I don't do it, who will? My mom, Alice Harper, taught me to look at what I can do, not what I can't. Everyone who volunteers in our community does that. I accept this award tonight in memory of my adoptive mother and on behalf of all the volunteers who work tirelessly throughout our community. Thank you." She raised the plaque high and smiled before she went back to her seat.

Event staff moved the tables aside to make room for dancing. When the band opened with a slow classic, Uncle Charles led her onto the floor for the first dance. The mayor and his wife, along with several other council members, joined them. As the next song began, Jeremy led Abby onto the dance floor, and Nick claimed Katherine's hand while the judge sought out Aunt Melvia.

"So, how does it feel to be the city's sweetheart?" Nick teased while he twirled her around the room.

"I don't know if I'm considered their sweetheart. I'm more the redheaded stepchild who hasn't shamed the family yet."

He frowned at her. "Why do you always do that?"

She'd meant it as a joke, but Nick's scowl meant that wasn't how he'd taken it. "Do what?"

"Why do you always sell yourself short? You're an amazing woman. You've accomplished so much and you did it through your own hard work, without anyone doing you any favors."

Their dance ended before she could answer. Jeremy claimed her hand and sent Nick off to dance with Abby. "I'm so proud of you. I know you don't like a lot of attention, but you're a public figure now." He beamed at her.

"Stop, Jeremy. You know I hate this sort of thing."

Being Citizen of the Year also meant she had to remain at the dinner until it ended. Katherine had danced more tonight than she had in her entire life. How could Nick want to do this on a regular basis? He and his future debutante wife could have it. She was exhausted. Her face hurt from all the smiling almost as much as her feet did thanks to the strap of her heeled sandal biting into the side of her toe.

It was late when Nick drove her home. "So, tell me how you know Abby."

"She and I both work with Big Sisters. Abby gets stuck with the administrative duties while I work with the girls directly."

"Does it bother you that Abby doesn't roll her sleeves up and get her hands dirty the way you do?"

"No. What Abby does brings in the funding for supplies and covers the cost of taking the girls on field trips. She deserved that award more than I did."

"Yeah, and she welcomes the attention more than you do, too," he teased, oblivious to her rising temper.

"She would make an ideal politician's wife, don't you think?" Her smile and tone were nothing but sugar.

Nick shrugged instead of taking the bait. "If that's what she wanted." He glanced over at her. "For someone who claims to be so in tune to who's perfect for whom, you sure miss some obvious signals."

"What are you talking about?"

"Jeremy."

"What about Jeremy?" she asked, still confused.

"I'm saying Abby has plans for Jeremy."

"No. Really?"

"Oh, yes. But Jeremy's too busy playing big brother to you. He's clueless about Abby's interest." Nick glanced her way. "Believe me; I play on his basketball team. He and I've been close friends for the past several years. He keeps his comments about Abby down to a suspicious minimum."

Nick's revelation of a strong friendship with Jeremy made her aware of how little he'd shared about himself. "You let me believe you'd never met."

"I didn't know how well you knew each other. A guy likes to scope out the competition before revealing too much."

They pulled into her driveway.

It took a few seconds for his words to register. She scrambled out of the door he'd opened for her. "Competition? For me?"

He shrugged in a helpless gesture and followed her up the walk and onto the porch.

"I assure you, you have nothing to worry about."

"Really?" The relief in his voice proved he'd missed the sarcasm.

She unlocked the door before she turned to cut him off at the knees. "I wouldn't date you if you were the last man on earth."

"What? Wait a second. You just said—"

"I know what I said. You made your opinion of me abundantly clear years ago. A fancy dress, a law degree, and a shiny award." She waved the plaque between them. "None of those things change my past or who I am. I'll always be a former foster kid. The kind of person you think you can use, then throw away like an old newspaper."

"Kat, what in the world are you talking about?" He stalled her with a hand on her arm.

"None of this makes me one of the right people you need to align yourself with to further your political career." Her heart pounded in her chest. "I wasn't good enough for you in high school. I'm sure not good enough for you now because I'm the same person inside." She snatched her arm free and slammed the door in his face.

Once inside, she slid to the floor in a heap. The thud of his fist against the solid wood matched the roar in her ears. She sat in the dark, ignoring his demands for her to open the door.

Where was the satisfaction? The pleasure of finally confronting him after all these years? All she felt was empty and alone. When she heard him drive away, she ran up the stairs and flung herself onto her bed. She buried her face in her pillow to muffle the sobs. The action was wasted. There was no one to hear her cries. No one at all. That made it hurt more. With the ache of loneliness heavy in the room, she promised herself this was the last time she shed a tear over Nick Delaney.

Chapter 7

Nick yelled Katherine's name and pounded on the front door for ten minutes before he gave up. He could imagine her neighbors peeking out their windows to see what was going on and calling the police. On top of everything else, being arrested was the last thing he needed tonight. Hurt and confused by her rejection, he made himself walk back to his car and drive home.

He spent the rest of Friday night in bed, flat on his back, staring at the ceiling. What had she meant? How had he used her? He'd asked her to tutor him. She'd agreed. He'd passed his entrance exam with her help and he'd said thank you, a lot, if he remembered correctly.

And then she'd vanished.

He replayed the conversation he'd had with her thirteen years ago. This time, hearing the words that had come out of his mouth instead of the ones he'd meant to say. The ones he'd practiced saying in front of the mirror before meeting her in the library. The ones that told her how much she meant to him. That he wouldn't have been able to succeed without her. How he wanted to stay in touch even though he was going away to school. *Ahhhh. I'm an idiot.*

As dawn peeped through the drapes, he stepped into

the shower, unable to stand the solitude of his bedroom a minute longer. He'd said the words he'd promised his father he would, and he'd hurt the first girl he'd let himself care about. Hurt her to the point she'd run away. He couldn't say anything that would make amends for the pain he'd caused her then or now.

His team had a game at nine. With any luck, it would keep his mind busy. He would talk to Jeremy, but not before the game. As protective as he was about Kat, Nick would be lucky if Jeremy didn't use him as a punching bag when he told him about this latest fiasco with Kat.

Their team won by twenty, thanks to him. He used the physicality of the game to work off some of his frustration.

"Man, you were vicious out there today," Jeremy said while they waited for their burgers at Maida's Café.

"Yeah, I needed a target." Nick shifted in his chair.

"Anything you want to talk about?"

Nick tried to avoid his eyes, but Jeremy waited him out.

"I think I know what I did that hurt Kat when we were in high school." He hung his head. "I let my mouth go faster than my head and basically said she wasn't the right kind of person for me to have around because I was going to be somebody."

"You what?" Several patrons at tables nearby turned and stared at the heated tone of the local pastor's voice.

Nick leaned forward and spoke in a hushed, but urgent whisper. "I didn't realize that's what came out of my mouth at the time. It wasn't what I meant to say. Look, I liked her. A lot. When my dad made me tell her I was leaving, it about ripped my heart out." Nick tried to make Jeremy understand how intense and churned up he'd been that awful day. That he felt the same way today, confessing what he'd done accidentally.

"So you made sure you sliced hers up in the process.

They say misery loves company." Jeremy gave him a disgusted look.

"Hey, you're supposed to be my friend, and a minister. You have to help me fix this," Nick pleaded, unable to hide the hurt Jeremy's words caused.

Jeremy stopped and bowed his head in prayer. Nick held his breath and waited, asking God to show him how to heal the rift he'd caused between himself and his friend, and the one between him and Kat.

Jeremy looked up and their eyes locked. "I'm sorry. Please forgive me for my harsh words." He offered a lopsided smirk. "How did you figure it out?"

"Kat sort of told me last night, right after she declared I was the last man on earth she'd ever go out with and slammed the door in my face."

Jeremy's shoulders shook, but he held the laugh inside. "She's stubborn and she has a fierce temper. I think you should go see Judge Pierce."

"Right, I'm sure he'd enjoy being the first family court judge to sentence someone to death." Agitated, Nick tried to reason with Jeremy and find another solution. "Look, I hurt her before and I'm pretty sure I made her cry last night. He won't be happy to see me."

"But he needs to know she's upset. Otherwise, he'll wonder what's causing all the tension in his courtroom Monday morning. You need to prepare him. He can help you make it less painful for her when she faces you in court."

Nick fought the urge to beat his head against the table. "And my dad wonders why I'm single."

"You appreciate things more if you have to work for them. That applies to relationships, too."

"I'm not going to get her. She all but hates me. I just want to help heal the wounds I've inflicted on her. She deserves to be loved by someone a lot better than me. Someone who will never hurt her."

"Come on. First, we have to figure out how to get her to talk to you so you can tell her how sorry you are. I'll go with you to see Judge Pierce. I'll even call him so he knows we're coming."

Nick ran home for a quick shower. On his way out, his phone rang.

"Hello."

"Hello. How was your game?"

"Hi, Dad. It was good."

"Did you win?"

"Yeah, we won."

"That Citizen of the Year, it's the foster kid isn't it?"

"Yeah, they're one and the same."

"I was right. She's nothing but trouble for you."

"No, Dad. You were wrong about her. Just look at all she's achieved. And it had nothing to do with knowing the right people. That makes her a lot better person than me in my book. She got where she is today by working hard. She didn't get any breaks. I don't want to fight with you about her right now, okay?"

"All right then. I called to tell you we're sending out the press release Monday."

"Monday? Why are you bumping it up?"

"Have you seen this morning's paper?"

"No, I haven't had time. Look, I have to go. I'll call you tonight and we can talk about the press release then."

After Nick got into his car, he reached for the newspaper he'd thrown in the backseat when he'd left for the game earlier. The front page of the community section sported a huge picture of him dancing with Kat. The caption read, "Council Hopeful Woos Pemberly's Top Citizen."

Great! She'll blame me for this, too. He tossed the paper

onto the seat. When he stopped to pick Jeremy up, he got in the car and presented Nick with another copy.

"Thanks, I already have one."

"Man, when you try to have a bad day, you go all out don't you?"

"Not funny."

"Judge Pierce has seen this, too."

"Terrific. Maybe we should turn around and go home now."

"He's seen it, but he hasn't talked to Katherine. For reasons I don't understand, I think he approves of you."

Nick caught the surprised look on Jeremy's face. "You don't have to sound so shocked at the idea. Most people do like me. I'm having a problem getting Kat to like me. And, after I tell Judge Pierce everything, he's not going to be a big fan either."

"I'm sure he'll give you the chance to explain everything. Then he'll kill you."

"You what?" Judge Pierce bellowed and jumped to his feet.

"I didn't realize that's what I said at the time. I definitely didn't mean it. She's very upset, sir. I want to make this right." Nick met the other man's furious glare head-on. "I have to."

"You better. And to think I shamed her into being nice to you last weekend." The judge paced in front of the cold hearth in his library.

After several minutes of silence that had Nick ready to climb the walls, the judge stopped and looked down his nose at him. "Well, what are you going to do about this, Mr. Delaney?"

"I don't know, yet. But I came here today to explain. I will make this up to her. I'll prove to her that isn't the way

I see her." Nick swallowed hard. "We, you and I, need to be as supportive as possible in the courtroom on Monday morning. Kat is strong, but she's wounded and those wounds run deep." And it about killed him to know *his* words had inflicted the pain. "I need your help." He met the judge's frigid glare.

"And why I should help you?"

"Because I don't want to ever see her hurt again. Give me a little time and I'll prove to her how sorry I am. I'll show her how much she means to me."

The judge searched his face, Nick assumed, to gauge the depth of his sincerity.

"Flowers might be a good start," the judge suggested.

"I sent her an orchid last Monday."

"What for?"

Jeremy laughed.

Nick's scowl silenced him. "To thank her for doing all the cooking."

"I imagine you'll need a lot more than an orchid if you stand any hope of climbing out of the canyon you've dug for yourself."

"That's it? Flowers? No other suggestions?" He looked at the judge in disbelief before he turned toward Jeremy.

Jeremy raised his hands in a helpless motion. "I only agreed to come with you. You have to fix this yourself. I'm her friend, too. Think of me as Switzerland."

Nick sat forward and rubbed his hands over his face. "God, help me."

"He's the only one who can," Jeremy muttered from beside him.

Katherine reached for the phone as she pulled her head out from under her pillow.

"'lo."

"Katherine?"

"Um-hm."

"It's Abby. Blackmon. Are you okay? Did I wake you?"

"Yeah, I'm fine," she said and sat up. "I didn't get to bed until late."

"I wanted to take you to lunch today. A sort of celebratory meal for your award."

"Okay. Where did you want to go?" She glanced at the clock on the nightstand.

"How about Dante's? They have an awesome strawberry salad."

"That sounds great. I'll meet you at noon."

In the bathroom, Katherine didn't glance at her reflection in the mirror. She stepped straight into the shower. The spray of hot water beat against her back, driving energy into her sluggish system. She lifted her face and let the hot pulses of water rinse away any residual puffiness from her crying jag. If it didn't work, concealer was a wonderful invention.

She and Abby arrived within minutes of each other. When she walked up, Abby hugged her. "I'm so glad you won. You give so much of yourself to the community. You're an amazing role model for the kids we help."

"Yeah, well, I'm kind of uncomfortable with people knowing what I do to help out."

"You better get used to it. You made the news last night." Abby caught the door and let her go in first.

The hostess showed them to a table, forcing Katherine to wait to respond. "What do you mean?"

Abby put the newspaper on the table in front of her and smiled. "You were the belle of the ball."

Katherine fought a wave of nausea. "I didn't know they were taking pictures." The pressure from the headache she had awakened with inched farther down her scalp and tightened the muscles in her neck and shoulders. She stared at the picture, remembering the warmth of Nick's hand at her waist. The smell of his cologne.

"I had no idea you and Nick were an item," Abby teased.

"We're not!"

"Uh-huh. And a man looks at a woman he has no feelings for with that kind of tenderness in his eyes."

"He wasn't showing tenderness. It was pity. We must have been talking about my childhood."

Abby gave her a baleful look. "You don't really believe that, do you?"

"There is absolutely nothing between us. Nick doesn't think someone like me would be good enough for him. He has this image in his mind of the perfect woman, and thank goodness I'm the complete opposite of that image."

"There's no way Nick doesn't think you're good enough. He is the least snobby guy I know." Then Abby threw Katherine's own concern back at her. "How would you feel if he thought you were too good for him?"

Katherine let out an inelegant snort and rolled her eyes. "I'm pretty sure Nick has a really high opinion of himself. There are very few women he would view as above him."

She watched Abby's eyes stray to the picture below the fold, in the corner of the page. The look on Abby's face as she danced with Jeremy.

"But I know sometimes guys are clueless about the perfect woman, even when she's right in front of them." Katherine's voice became earnest.

Sadness dulled the sparkle in Abby's eyes when she glanced up. "You're lucky you understood your calling to public service so young. I didn't discover mine until a few years ago. I met a man who challenges me to do more, to be more than I ever thought I could. But he thinks I'm so far above him, I'm out of reach. It makes me want to scream sometimes." Abby took her frustration out on the loaf of bread the waiter had left for them. Her nervous fingers turned the mound into a mangled heap of crumbs. "He treats me like a paragon while I think he's the finest man I've ever known."

So Nick was right about Jeremy and Abby. "Well, maybe we should find a way to make him see you in a different light. We could make him jealous." Katherine shot her a devious grin.

"You don't even know who he is," Abby balked.

Katherine pointed to the picture of Abby and Jeremy. "Who's the dreamy-eyed one there?"

Abby leaned forward. "Do you play tennis?"

"Not since high school gym glass."

"How would you like to use some tennis balls as target practice?"

Katherine couldn't help but grin.

"So how do we make Jeremy see me in a new light?" Abby asked her an hour later as they volleyed the ball back and forth over the net on the tennis courts at the YMCA.

Katherine welcomed the distraction of playing cupid to take her mind off Nick and the jumble of feelings that surged through her at the mention of his name. "How often do you see him?"

"When my father's in town, he invites Jeremy to lunch with us after Sunday services. And I volunteer at the food bank and clothes closet at the church. So, I guess I see him three or four times a week."

Katherine paused, and a ball sailed past. "Why don't you call him and invite him to dinner?"

"I could do that." Abby spun her racket in her hand. "Or even ask him to a movie. He plays basketball. His team practices on Mondays and Thursdays."

"When are their games?"

"On Saturday mornings. I guess we missed today's." Abby sounded disappointed. "Hey, you can come with me. That way it won't be so obvious."

"I don't think that's a good idea."

"Why not? Nick plays on the same team."

She aimed her racket at Abby. "That would be why."

"I know you said he doesn't care for you, but you guys act okay around each other. I don't understand." Abby caught the ball in her hand, walked over to the bench beside the court and sat down. She gave Katherine a challenging look.

Katherine had no choice but to sit beside her. "It's a front. Nick and I, well, we don't get along." She fingered the strings of her racket and avoided Abby's gaze.

"Are you crazy? He couldn't take his eyes off you last night. Besides, weren't you his date?"

"No! He only brought me as a favor to Uncle Charles. How do I make you understand this? Nick is using me to score brownie points with the judge while he's stuck in family court."

"And you believe that?"

"He's done it before."

"I've got all day." Abby tapped the face of her watch. "Go ahead, spell it out for me."

Maybe the aftereffects of the emotional roller coaster she'd ridden last night, or the sympathetic tone Abby inflected in her question, or the desperate need for a friend were to blame. She'd never told anyone of the betrayal she'd experienced at the hands of the Delaneys. Katherine took a deep breath. "We went to high school together. I tutored him and once he had a higher test score, he had his father send me packing."

Abby sat in stunned silence. "I wouldn't have pictured

Nick as a user. His father is always trying to get ahead, but I thought Nick was a nice guy. I still can't believe it. He acts like he's nuts about you," Abby argued.

"He's trying to schmooze Uncle Charles."

"Nick cares for you. I know he does. I agree you have cause not to trust him. But you fight against making assumptions about people every day. You make the system hear those kids' stories before they make decisions about their futures. Doesn't Nick deserve the same opportunity? At least consider it." She reached over and squeezed Katherine's hand. "I'd feel so much better if you came with me next Saturday, but I don't want you to be uncomfortable."

"I'll think about it. I promise." As they walked to their cars, she smiled at Abby. "So, are you going to ask Jeremy out this week or not?"

Abby sighed. "I'm really nervous. I can talk to him all night about programs for the church. But what do I say to him that doesn't relate to that? I want him to see me outside the role of volunteer."

"Then ask him to a movie. There won't be as much time for talking. He's definitely interested in you. You just need to get his attention."

"Okay, but if he acts like I've gone off the deep end, I'm sending you to talk to him."

"Go ahead. I'd love to set him straight."

As Abby backed out of the parking lot, she called out, "Good luck in court Monday. Think about what I said."

Katherine waved her off, but was too edgy to go home, so she took a chance and went to Uncle Charles and Aunt Melvia's house. The dogs were out front playing when she drove up. As soon as she got out of her car, they were all over her, begging for attention.

Uncle Charles rose from a chair on the porch. "What an honor to receive a personal visit from our favorite citizen."

"Cut it out. That was a sneaky thing you did to me last night." She hugged him.

"That was all I could come up with to get you there so I could present you with the award." He walked her inside to the kitchen, where Aunt Melvia was snapping beans. She wiped her hands before giving Katherine a warm hug.

"You were so beautiful last night. No one deserved that award more than you did. We love you very much." She held Katherine away from her and wiped the twin tears as they streamed down Katherine's cheeks.

"I love you both, too." She managed around the sudden lump in her throat.

"Will you stay for dinner?" Aunt Melvia asked.

"Sure, how can I help?"

"There's nothing left. Go visit with Charles while I finish up in here," Melvia ordered and shooed her out of the kitchen and down the hall.

Katherine found him in his study. His intense gaze followed her as she took her usual spot on the sofa near his chair.

"Why are you looking at me so hard? I'm the same person I was before they gave me the award."

"That's not what I'm looking at. How's your heart?"

Her smile froze on her face. "My heart's fine. Why?"

"I had a visit from Nick today."

"Oh? I wouldn't have thought he'd want to spend two weekends in a row with you."

"That won't work with me, young lady," he scolded. "What happened last night?"

She got up and moved over in front of the fireplace, rearranging the miniature teacups displayed on the mantle. "He asked me about dating him and I told him I wasn't interested." She glanced back, trying to gauge his reaction.

He kept his expression blank. "I heard your answer was a little more impassioned than a simple 'no thank you.'"

Her shoulders sagged. She was so tired. "I told him no in a way that ensured he won't ask me again."

"Why?"

"Isn't it enough that he hurt me a long time ago and it still hurts?"

"Maybe it still hurts because he still means something to you."

She shook her head. "That was a long time ago. I hadn't thought of him in years, not until he showed up in court. I don't want to care about him. I'm fine without him."

"Do you really believe that? If he stirs this many emotions in you…"

"He doesn't." And she would never let him.

Chapter 8

A storm blew through on Sunday night, leaving Monday morning damp and gloomy. A perfect match for Katherine's mood. She drove straight to the courthouse instead of swinging by her office first. Traffic crawled, adding to her frustration. She was late. She hated being late. She rushed into the courtroom. Uncle Charles and Nick both paused as she took her seat.

"Miss Harper, everything okay?"

"Everything's fine. The weather has traffic snarled on my side of town."

"Today's hearing addresses the status of Stevie Mills and his care." The judge swiveled his head toward her. "What is his grandmother's prognosis?"

"Mrs. Tindle is fully recovered, and Dr. Collins has released her from the rehab center. He foresees no problems with her assuming care of Stevie. I will follow up monthly and make sure she and Stevie are doing fine, but I don't expect any problems."

"That's good news. Mr. Delaney, do you have any questions?"

"No, sir. I'm happy to hear Mrs. Tindle is better so she and Stevie can be together."

Uncle Charles tapped his gavel on the padded block, signaling the close of the case. He dismissed the session and left Katherine alone with Nick in the courtroom without a backward glance. It was a setup if ever she saw one.

Nick moved toward her as she placed her files inside her briefcase. "Katherine, may I speak with you, please?"

She met his gaze and nodded.

"I wanted to tell you I'm sorry for the things I said to you in the library that day back in high school. The words that came out of my mouth then were not the ones I meant to say. I don't think I'm better than anyone, especially not you."

He looked so humble, so full of contrition.

"In fact, I've always thought you were one of the best people I know. I admired you then and I admire you even more now. There is no way to make up for the pain I've caused you, but I wanted to give you this." He handed her a black velvet box.

Her tongue had tied itself in a knot that matched the one in her stomach. She took the box with unsteady hands. When the hinged lid snapped open, she gasped. Winking back at her, outlined in gold wire were clusters of bronze-colored stones that created the coat of a golden retriever with sparkling black eyes.

A rushing, burning sensation flowed through her. "He's beautiful." She ran her finger over the stones.

"You said you're never home so a real dog is out of the question. It was this or a stuffed toy and I didn't want you to have to fight one of the kids over him." He reached for the box, freeing the pin from its clasp, and waited for her permission before he fastened the brooch to the lapel of her suit jacket.

"I don't know what to say."

"There's nothing for *you* to say. I'm the one apologizing."

"Oh, well, um, thank you."

"You're very welcome." Nick turned and left her standing alone in the courtroom.

Katherine used the drive back to her office to clear away the fog swirling in her mind over Nick's whimsical, yet perfect, peace offering. A glimpse at her face in the rearview mirror reflected a goofy smile she couldn't wipe away. She was pathetic if a piece of costume jewelry affected her like this.

When she opened the outer door to her office, Gina pounced. "Thank the Lord. I've been going absolutely insane here. Ah-choo!"

The edge in the unflappable Gina's voice jolted Katherine into the here and now. Her mission-style furnished reception area had become a massive sea of floral arrangements. Every available surface held a giant vase overflowing with roses in every color of the rainbow and then some.

The sweet heady fragrance drew her in, wrapping her senses in a deluge of spring images. "Bless you. What happened?" She tried to find somewhere to set her briefcase.

"Mr. Nicolas Delaney is what happened," Gina stated in an odd combination of admiration flavored with a hint of vexation. "Ah-choo. I had to start lining them up along the wall because I'd put a vase on every flat surface in here with the first round of deliveries." Gina sneezed again into a tissue.

"There was more than one delivery?"

"Every hour, on the hour. A different florist backs an oversized van up to the front door and makes ten trips in carrying these beauties. What is he apologizing for?"

"How do you know he's apologizing?" she asked, shocked at Gina's acuity.

"Honey, no man sends this many roses unless he's in

deep trouble." Her arms encompassing the whole room, Gina gave her a condescending look. "Judging by the quantity delivered today, he must have offended the entire female population of the state."

Katherine peeked into her office. A mass of vases topped three corners of her desk. Rose petals and baby's breath overshadowed the orchid on her credenza. She looked back at Gina and found her standing in the middle of the room with her arms folded across her chest, her toe tapping—waiting.

"Well?" Gina demanded.

"You remember me saying I knew Nick in high school?"

"Uh-huh. Go on," Gina prompted with her nose buried in a tissue.

"He said some things that hurt me back then. I think he's saying he's sorry."

Gina stared at her in disbelief. "He's doing all this to say he's sorry for hurting your feelings thirteen years ago?"

"I've sort of been holding a grudge." She fingered the velvety petal of a crimson rose before leaning down and sampling its fragrance.

"Is he forgiven?"

She inhaled deeply, enjoying the sweet smell as she thought over her answer. "He's getting there," she murmured and strolled into her office, leaving Gina to handle any more deliveries.

She had to call him. At the very least, to thank him, and to tell him to stop before Gina deserted her. She worried about what was happening and what this softening around her heart meant as she looked at the beautiful flowers and touched the brooch he'd pinned to her jacket. Every time she turned around, he came at her with something new, knocking her off balance again. He confused her, left her head spinning, wondering which way was up.

She understood holding on to words said years ago was petty, especially since he'd apologized so lavishly. But she was used to their bitter taste, almost immune to their bite. The feelings of resentment and hurt they stirred were familiar, their sharpness worn down by age.

The forgiveness Jeremy had preached about, and Abby had encouraged her to try, was harder to do. If she let the past go, what would take its place? Would there be a big open void, leaving her empty inside?

She needed control of her life, her emotions. She wouldn't rely on anyone else for her happiness. Everyone left her. Or in Nick's case, sent her away. That truth helped her keep her perspective and maintain her distance when she picked up the phone.

Her gratitude and request to lighten up were easier to express than she'd expected. She and Nick laughed over Gina's reaction, but Katherine held part of herself back, not able to forget his deepest betrayal. That, she didn't think she could ever forgive.

Later in the afternoon, Gina buzzed her to find out if she was available for Corinne Hightower, chairperson of the Businesswomen of Pemberly Coalition.

"Great, I'll send her in."

Katherine had three seconds to wonder why Corinne had stopped by before Gina ushered her through the door. She smiled and rose from her desk, offering her hand, but had to wait. The endless displays of floral arrangements at their finest managed to leave even Corinne speechless.

"Sorry about this," Katherine began, indicating the sea of bouquets. "I seem to have an overzealous fan."

"I'll say. They're gorgeous. He has excellent taste."

"Please, have a seat. What can I do for you?"

Corinne regained her focus and offered her a sly smile.

"Actually, Miss Harper, it's what the Businesswomen of Pemberly can do for you."

"I'm sorry, you've lost me."

"We want to sponsor you as our candidate for the open city council seat."

"Me? But I've never been interested in politics."

"Maybe not, but you are very interested in this community, Miss Citizen of the Year."

"Yes, well, I don't do volunteer work for awards or to get elected to public office. I do it to help people."

Corinne leaned forward. "I know. It's what makes you an ideal candidate. You love this community. You want to help people, and as a council member, you would have a chance to shape policy by creating programs and voting on agendas that would help even more people than you can reach as a volunteer.

"There are only two women on the eight-seat council right now. The Coalition thinks more women need to be in a position to offer ideas and changes. To shift the balance of power."

After the initial shock, Katherine found her voice and pointed out a flaw in Corinne's presentation. "That's fine and good, but I would never agree to run for office just because I'm a woman and you want to change the status quo."

"But you would consider running if it meant making a difference. You have a burden in your heart for the disadvantaged. Who else on the council feels that burden like you do?"

"But Nick Delaney…" It was out of her mouth before she could stop it.

"A rich man's son?" Corinne countered. "How in tune to the needs of this community would he be?"

"He—"

Corinne held up a hand to stall her. "All I'm asking you

to do is give the idea some thought. I'll drop by next week and you can give me your answer then."

Stunned, Katherine could only nod and mumble her consent to the open-ended follow-up.

Gina stopped in the doorway of her office and leaned against the doorjamb, taking in her shell-shocked stillness. "So, what did Miss Mover and Shaker want?"

"They want me to run for city council."

Gina abandoned all propriety and flopped down in the chair facing her, her mouth open. "No way!"

"Yes, way. They think there aren't enough women in power and I would have the community's best interests at heart."

"Are you?"

"Am I what?"

"Going to run?"

"I don't know. I mean, no. Absolutely not. I have no political aspirations. That's Nick's domain," she explained, wondering why it wasn't obvious to Gina.

"I see. You don't want to go head to head against Nicky Boy. You're afraid he'll beat you."

"Oh, please. Nick has nothing to do with this. I mean, with me running for office. I don't want to be on the council."

"Did you tell Corinne that?"

"Yes."

"And she said, 'okay, thanks anyway,' right?"

Katherine gave Gina a squinted glare. "She asked me to think about it and let her know."

"Will you?"

"How can I not think about it now that she's asked me such a crazy thing? It'll be like that 'The Wheels on the Bus' song playing in my head for the next week."

"Well, I'm calling Judge Pierce." Gina sprang from her seat, already on her way to the door.

"Don't you dare," Katherine ordered. "He doesn't need to know about this. He'd worry for nothing."

"Trust me. It will go better for you if he hears about this from you instead of Corinne at some country club luncheon later this week."

"You think she would do that?"

"Are you kidding me? The Coalition finally has their poster child, or should I say, woman. They'll be champing at the bit to get you to agree to run. Prepare to be seriously courted between now and her follow-up visit next week."

Katherine hadn't put much stock in Gina's warning about political wooing. However, the growing stack of invitations to luncheons and dinners cluttering her desk gave support to the prediction and changed her social life from nonexistent to nonstop overnight.

The luncheons were easy to brush off. After all, she had a full-time day job. The dinners, however, left her feeling guilty when she declined. Not all of them were to get her to run for office. Some were congratulations for the Citizen of the Year Award.

Oh, how she missed the days before she received that annoying award. She picked out three invitations she knew she couldn't ignore. All three were from Uncle Charles.

"There's nothing to think about. I have no interest in politics," she told Abby over lunch two days after the meeting. She'd just given her all the details of Corinne's offer.

"I don't know," Abby speculated. "Corinne brought up some valid arguments. This could be an opportunity to help a lot more people within the community than you can right now. This would give you a platform for your charity work."

"You're serious. You think I should run?"

Abby used her fork to flake the crust from around her quiche and kept her eyes on her plate. "I think you'd be great at the job. I know you'd be fair and wouldn't let outside interests sway you like some people would."

"Are you willing to sign on as my campaign manager if I do?"

"If you decided to run, I'd do all I could to get you elected."

"Even go against Nick?"

Abby dismissed the question with a wave of her fork. "Nick isn't the only one who cares about this community."

"I still don't think I'm the best person for the job."

"Give it more time. Corinne won't call until next week. Are you coming to the dinner for the children's wing dedication at the hospital tonight?"

Katherine gave her a tired smile. "Yes, I have to go. Uncle Charles worked it out for me to cut the ribbon due to my celebrity status, of course."

"Of course." They both burst out laughing.

"I bet he's thrilled."

"Oh, you have no idea. I'm sure he's working on my acceptance speech right now."

"Maybe you should give the idea of running some serious thought."

She sighed. "I'm trying to keep an open mind. I've never pictured myself in the political arena."

"I trust you to make the right decision." Abby glanced at her watch. "I have to go. I have an afternoon meeting. I'll see you tonight." She squeezed Katherine's hand and left.

Katherine dressed for the ribbon cutting that evening without any jitters. She was going solo and would be with her small group of friends and Uncle Charles. No Nick.

At least not until she drove into the parking garage at

the hospital. The available spot she found was right next to a black BMW with the license plate NICKD2.

"Great." She climbed out of her car as the butterflies lined up for takeoff inside her stomach. With her luck, he'd be holding the door when she walked in.

Inside, the hospital cafeteria had been transformed into a fall festival complete with booths offering face painting, balloon animals, caricature drawings and even a fish tank. The young patients well enough to attend were having a ball. Their laughter and squeals echoed off the walls.

Their excitement tugged a smile from her. She wandered around, hoping to run into Uncle Charles since he said she'd be sitting with them. The one person she wanted to bump into less than Nick was Corinne Hightower. She spotted her dressed in a red power suit, chatting away with—Nick.

"Katherine, I didn't expect to see you again so soon. I was telling Mr. Delaney he might not be a shoo-in for the council seat he's after."

Katherine met Nick's gaze. "Corinne, I haven't had time to think about your offer."

"I didn't realize you had political aspirations." Nick threw her words back at her.

"I don't, or I didn't. But Corinne presented some good arguments. I agreed to at least consider their request." She wasn't deceiving him. Entertaining the offer was a long way from entering the race.

"If you'll excuse me, my father just arrived."

Corinne watched him walk away before turning back to Katherine. "I think you make him nervous."

"The feeling's mutual. Corinne, I have to go find Uncle Charles. Excuse me." Katherine kept her pace casual, resisting the urge to cut and run.

Uncle Charles squeezed her hand when she stepped beside him. "Hello dear. I'd like you to meet Senator Harold Blackmon."

"Senator, it's a pleasure to meet you."

"Congratulations on your award. Our community could use more citizens like you."

"Thank you, but there are so many volunteers doing more than I ever could. And most of them go unrecognized for their hard work."

"True. But think of the influence you would have to change that as a council member," the senator said.

Katherine turned an accusing glare on her uncle. He held his hands up in mock surrender.

"Don't blame him," the senator said. "I saw Abby this afternoon. She thinks it's a great idea. You have a campaign manager whether you run or not."

A ball of tension planted itself in her stomach and bounced its way up into her chest at the mention of the council seat. Hoping to change the subject, she looked around. When she didn't find her wannabe campaign manager, she asked, "Where is Abby?"

"Oh, she's riding with Pastor Walker." He checked his watch. "They should be here any minute."

She glanced at the door in time to see Jeremy enter with Abby draped on his arm. He spotted them and led Abby in their direction. He offered a warm welcome to her father when they reached the group.

"Well, well, well, Pastor Walker. Fancy seeing you here," Katherine teased.

Jeremy glanced at Abby before responding. "She can be very persuasive."

"Stop it. You got an invitation in the mail like the rest of us. I know because I addressed it myself."

Jeremy shook his head. "All she had to say was she needed someone to make sure she behaved. It's what I do."

Abby gaped at him. "I cannot believe you said that, and in front of my father."

Senator Blackmon threw his head back and roared with laughter, then looked at Jeremy with interest. "I think you've met your match, Abby. Pastor Walker won't put up with any foolishness."

Katherine and Abby took a stroll toward the buffet. Abby waited until she had a plate and napkin in her hands before casually asking if she'd seen Nick.

She grimaced. "Corinne Hightower had him cornered when I came in. She took great pleasure in letting him know they want to sponsor me."

"Oh, brother. How did he take it?"

"The temperature in here fell to below freezing based on the icy glare he hit me with. He excused himself to go speak with his father."

"You poor thing, I guess the truce is over."

"Ours was more like a temporary cease-fire."

"Come on. Daddy and Judge Pierce need us over by the stage. The ceremony can't officially start without our star citizen there with her scissors."

Senator Blackmon gave a short speech dedicating the new wing and the special pediatric medical equipment. Abby handed Katherine the oversized scissors and watched while she made the snip. Streamers and candy rained down all over the room. The children went wild.

"The nurses on duty tonight should ask for hazard pay," Katherine said to Senator Blackmon before easing along the wall away from the main cluster of scrambling kids.

"Leaving so soon?" A harsh voice stopped her in her tracks.

Startled, she looked up. Edward. He might have taken her by surprise, but he wouldn't intimidate her. "Mr. Delaney, it's been a while."

"Miss Jenkins." Before she could correct him, he held up his hand. "A rose by any other name is still one. And I suppose your entry into the council race is because you think some do-gooder award makes you qualified. You don't have the polish, the skills to represent this city. You're an orphan."

She'd never understood how Nick could send her away. But hearing the contempt this man—Nick's father—had for her, even after all these years…she knew he would have done anything to keep her away from Nick.

Suddenly she saw what she hadn't been able to see as a heartbroken teenager. Edward, not Nick, was the one with the motive and the means to carry out his own agenda. The one with enough disregard to treat her as if she were nothing.

Because that was what she was to him—nothing.

"It was your signature at the bottom of the touching letter to the regional director requesting my transfer so I could attend those special painting classes. You wrote about my dream to become a painter after I graduated, except I would be out of the system with no money to pay for training. I had no idea you cared, much less knew, about my dreams." The syrup she infused into her tone for a dream she'd never dreamed was at odds with the fury heating her blood to boiling.

"Nick said you'd changed." His gaze inspected her from head to toe. "You don't look anything like that timid bookworm I remember. But looks can be deceiving. You don't have the connections or the experience to run this city."

"Oh, Edward, you haven't changed a bit. Still as myopic and condescending as ever. You must consider me a threat to Nick's campaign to acknowledge my existence now."

"Corinne Hightower has been making the rounds tonight, using an act of charity to brew dissension within our community."

At her silence, he continued his probing of the old wounds scarring her heart. "This town might give you a worthless little do-gooder award, but they aren't about to trust their future to a thrown-away orphan, no matter what family finally felt sorry for her and gave her their name."

"There you are, Katherine." Abby glided up beside her with Jeremy in tow. "I've been looking all over for you. Daddy needs you for a photo op."

Abby turned and met Edward's sneer with pursed lips. "I know Katherine will be Nick's toughest competition if she decides to run, but you really should leave the debating to them. We wouldn't want the community to think you live your life vicariously through your son." Abby hooked arms with her and they walked away with Jeremy.

"Remind me to never make you mad. You're a force to be reckoned with," Katherine said.

"You have nothing to worry about. Nick's dad has always been a bully. Tonight, when the focus should be on helping sick children get well, he can go somewhere else to flex his evil muscles."

"How do you know Nick's father, Katherine?" Jeremy watched her.

"He was my advocate while I lived here."

"He approved your transfer so close to graduation?"

"I was one less file on his desk." Katherine closed her eyes in a silent prayer, asking God for peace. Taking a deep breath, she slowed Jeremy and Abby. "Look, it's been a crazy few days for me. I'm going to cut out early, okay?"

Abby hugged her. "You're still coming with me Saturday."

Katherine dreaded another meeting with Nick. "All right."

Jeremy eyed them both with a look of apprehension. "Should I be worried?"

Abby's throaty laugh faded as she led Jeremy over to where her father was holding court with Judge Pierce. Katherine inched her way through the crowd toward the exit.

In the garage, she looked up and saw Nick leaning against his car, waiting.

"Hi."

"Hi." Her steps faltered. "Were you waiting for me?"

"Yeah, I saw you talking to my dad. I figured you might be upset."

"Why would you think that?" She wasn't up to a game of twenty questions tonight. Her feet hurt, and she was tired.

"Considering the amount of steam coming out of his ears after I told him you might run for city council, it's a safe guess he wasn't nice to you."

She shrugged. As much as she disliked Edward, he was still Nick's father and she wouldn't come between them. And she realized Nick had probably been in this same spot all those years ago. He wasn't responsible for his father's actions. A bit of the weight pressing down on her soul lifted.

"I'm sorry," he said simply.

"For what? You didn't do anything." And she meant it.

"I've been wracked with guilt knowing what I said made you leave school."

"It's okay. You sent me flowers, gave me this cute dog." She fingered the brooch pinned to her lapel.

"You've forgiven me?"

She sucked in a deep breath. "Yes, I have. I've held on to that anger and resentment for so long, it's strange having it gone. I'm a little unsteady without it anchoring me. Give me some time to adjust."

"That's fair. I can wait."

Were they talking about the same thing? "Can you?"

He shook his head, "That's not what I meant. How about we change the subject?"

"Okay."

"We keep ending up at the same places, around the same people these days."

"It's a fluke. Things will go back to normal soon."

"Not if you run for office. We'll be thrown together at every turn."

She swallowed hard. "Are you thinking of adding me to your list of debutantes or trying to get me to back out of running against you?"

He raised a brow. "I don't know, maybe both. You said I need someone who knows how to cook."

Choosing the safer half of her question, she kept their discussion on politics. "I haven't agreed to run. I'm just thinking about it."

"I don't understand why you would want to. It will eat into your volunteer time."

"I know, but Corinne pointed out how I could use the seat to bring more attention to the disadvantaged in our community."

"They aren't the only ones you'll have to think about though. You'll have to worry about the businesses, the homeowners and the city workers. You'll have to find ways to pay for any programs you recommend. You can't pick favorites."

"Are you trying to talk me out of it? Afraid I could take you?"

"Oh no, I'd actually enjoy the challenge of running against you."

"Would you?" She was more interested in his answer than she wanted to be.

He offered her a lazy grin. "I find the idea of arguing— excuse me—debating with you, on ideals and your position on matters regarding the city's growth and development, very appealing. I love watching you champion something you believe in and the spark of passion that makes you glow in the courtroom when we disagree."

The coaxing softness of his voice added to the pale lighting of the garage, had the butterflies fluttering in her stomach and her knees wobbling. She placed her hand on the back of her car for balance.

"What are you trying to say?"

He cleared his throat as if dragging his focus back to their conversation. "You're an intelligent and expressive debater. I would find the race against you very stimulating. If I won, it would be because the people believe I can do the job better than someone I know and respect."

"Oh." Why did he have to be nice to her while she was reeling from her encounter with his father?

"Oh? I tell you how much I admire you and all you can say is 'oh'? Obviously, you don't see me as much of a threat. You sure know how to crush a guy's ego."

She shook her head to clear it. She needed to go home and pray. Ask God what she should do. Sparring with Nick, alone, in a parking garage, over whether or not she should run for office was not how she'd envisioned her evening ending.

"Look, it's been a long day and I'm all argued out. I need to go."

He pushed away from his car and stepped closer to her. Reaching out, he tucked a strand of hair behind her ear. "Okay, I'll see you Saturday."

The warm glide of his fingers as they skimmed over her cheek drove away some of the iciness of his father's venom. She blinked a few times before Nick's words seeped into her tired mind. "Saturday?"

His smile turned smug. "Abby called me to find out the

time for the game on Saturday. I wouldn't tell her unless she fessed up to her motive. She said she's bringing you. Have lunch with me after the game?"

"I can't."

"Can't or won't?"

She expelled a prayer along with her breath. "I don't want to date you."

"You said you've forgiven me. How better to prove it?"

She opened and closed her mouth, but nothing came out.

He smiled in triumph. "Great. Let Abby pick you up and I'll take you home."

Chapter 9

On the drive to the gym Saturday morning, Abby was as perky as a high school cheerleader. She wore a Panthers T-shirt with her jeans and tennis shoes. Katherine smiled and shook her head at her friend's obvious excitement.

"Are you trying out for the pep squad?" she teased.

"Me? No, I just want Jeremy to know I'm there for him."

"I'm pretty sure he'll know when we show up for the game."

"So why did you change your mind about going?"

"Well, I sort of…" Katherine hated the nervousness in her voice and let out a frustrated growl. "I'm having lunch with Nick." She scrambled out of the car the second they stopped, leaving Abby behind with a stunned look on her face.

Abby caught up with her before Katherine made it to the sidewalk. A big grin on her face, she set the alarm with her key fob. "I see. You know, if you keep spending time with him, I might think you're falling into 'like' with him."

Katherine stopped dead. "That is not what lunch is about. He caught me at a weak moment and I couldn't think of a valid excuse to get out of going."

"See, you're already thinking of his feelings. It proves you have a soft spot in your heart for him."

Katherine shivered, or convulsed, at the thought. "We are here today to promote you and your opportunities to snare the attention of Pastor Jeremy Walker, remember? Leave me and Nick out of it."

"I'm only playing." Abby draped an arm around her shoulder as they went inside.

Both teams were warming up on the court when they walked in. Abby took the lead and aimed for the far side of the gym, where a large group of Panthers fans were sitting. They found a couple of open seats right behind the team bench and sat down to watch the warm-up. There were several young women wearing Panther T-shirts. They waved pom-poms in the team colors whenever one of the players passed in front of them.

Katherine looked at Abby. "I had no idea church league men's basketball had such a following."

"It probably has something to do with the team claiming the two most eligible bachelors in town as starters." Abby frowned at the self-appointed cheerleaders.

"If you nab Jeremy, it should cut the fan base by half. That will make Nick's search for the perfect debutante easier."

"What makes you think Nick's after a debutante?"

The sting of a blush heated Katherine's cheeks. "Well, I assume that's the type of wife he wants. You know, to go with the good breeding, able to host a dinner party…" Her voice faded as she went on, and she squirmed under Abby's questioning gaze.

"You think that's what he wants in a wife? Honey, if that were his type, he wouldn't be single. The well-to-do mothers of Pemberly have been parading their daughters in front of him since he came home from college. They're not his type at all."

Chastened, Katherine didn't ask what his type was. It wasn't any of her business. She didn't need to know. It was definitely better if she didn't. So why wasn't he married? Abby's comments made sense, and they left her wondering.

A buzzer sounded. The team came over to the bench for some last-minute advice from their coach. Nick grinned when he spotted them. He nudged Jeremy and motioned with his head in their direction. Jeremy's look of surprise was priceless. Abby shrugged. Katherine waved.

Both teams played with surprising skill considering their amateur status, but Katherine kept her appreciation to herself. During the second half of the game, a player on the other team fouled Jeremy with an elbow to the face, or the nose, to be exact. He ran off the court with his hand over his face as another player rushed to replace him.

They gasped when he pulled his hand away and blood poured from his nose. Abby jumped over the empty seats in front of them and was at his side when the team doctor reached him. Dr. Carter checked the injury and handed him an ice pack.

Abby sat next to Jeremy, rubbing her hand over his back, for the last five minutes of the game. Katherine went back to her seat alone. The Panthers won by six thanks to Nick and some aggressive rebounding. He headed straight for her as soon as the game ended, glancing at Jeremy to make sure he was okay as he jogged by. Jeremy nodded before casting an embarrassed look at Abby and her fawning attentions.

"Hi."

"Good game."

He flopped down next to her while he caught his breath. "Yeah, except for that guy taking Jeremy out. But he looks to be in good hands." He wiped his sweaty face with a towel.

"I think he has himself a nurse even if the doctor didn't order one. It's a good thing she isn't my ride home. I'd be in the way."

He reached out and squeezed her hand. The cheerleaders had moved closer. He glanced up and they smiled. "Thanks for cheering us on. It means a lot to the team." He smiled back before he scooted closer to her. "This is my friend Katherine."

The trio of cheerleaders looked her up and down before offering a reluctant greeting.

"Nice to meet you. I love your pom-poms." They gave her a confused look before they walked away.

Nick's low chuckle in her ear sent goose bumps trailing down her arm. "Now that was subtle."

She slid away, needing a little distance. "The oldest one can't be twenty yet."

"I'm not going to ask one of them out on a date. It is nice to have people in the stands cheer for us while we play, though. And since they're over eighteen, I might win their vote."

"Oh, please. Let's go check on Jeremy before we leave."

He followed her over to Jeremy and Abby.

"Are you okay?"

Jeremy cut his eyes toward Abby and stood up. "Yes, I'm fine. Abby flips out at the sight of blood."

"I did not flip out. I was worried about you. You were bleeding, a lot."

"I'm fine now." Jeremy shook his head at them.

"All right, we believe you." Nick held his hands up. "Since you feel so fine, do you two want to join us for lunch?"

They both shook their heads, no.

"Your loss." Nick reached for his gym bag and offered his hand to Katherine.

She stared at his open palm for a few seconds before placing hers in his grasp. She threw a nervous look over her shoulder at Abby as Nick led her out of the gym.

He held the car door for her then stowed his bag in the trunk. He hesitated before starting the car. "Do you mind if we swing by my apartment? I'd really like to grab a shower before we go eat." When she started to answer, he cut her off. "Ten minutes tops, I promise. With Jeremy out the last part of the game, I had to play longer than usual. I feel extra grungy."

She hesitated, taking in his soaked T-shirt and wet hair. "Sure, and I'll give you fifteen minutes if you need it."

They pulled into the underground parking garage of a twelve-story glass-encased complex. His apartment was on the top floor. In the elevator, she reminded herself today was about proving they'd moved on, that she'd forgiven him. And she had.

"We're here." He unlocked his door and let her step inside, before motioning her toward the living room. "Make yourself at home. I'll be right back."

After Katherine heard the shower running, she got up and wandered around the room, admiring his photos. Nick with his father at graduation. Nick and what looked like Jeremy with a trophy blocking his face, and one of Nick at a Boys and Girls Club function.

A few minutes later, his house phone rang, startling her away from the windows overlooking the park across the street. His machine clicked on after the fourth ring, his casual tone asking the caller to leave a message filled the room.

"Son, I don't think cozying up to the little orphan girl is the way to convince her not to run against you. Call me when you get in. We need to meet with Jeff tomorrow and come up with a strategy to neutralize her before she can do any real damage to your campaign."

Katherine stared at the blinking light on the machine, Edward's words reviving the anger she thought she was free of after she'd forgiven Nick. But the truth was clear and it was ugly. His father had put Nick in the middle again. Edward would force Nick to choose between her and him. She was never anyone's first choice. Nothing had changed.

Edward would always try to control Nick's life. And Nick would let him, because he loved his father and was blind to the hate that lived in his father's heart. She had to stop him. She was the only one who could. The loss of what might have been before it had a chance to start doubled her over in pain.

She would never ask Nick to choose between them because family should come first. She fought for that every day. She was frantic to escape, before she changed her mind and did something selfish that could create an eternal rift between Nick and Edward.

Nick picked that moment to come out of the bedroom dressed in jeans, a polo shirt, and sneakers. He took one look at her and led her to the couch. "What's wrong? What happened?"

She shook her head, squeezing her eyes shut against the stinging tears, and prayed for strength. "Nothing, I…" She swallowed past the lump of sorrow in her throat. This hurt as much as watching them lower Alice's casket into the ground. "I need to go home. I don't feel well."

"Are you sure? Is there anything I can do?" He reached for her.

She jerked away from him and moved toward the door. "No, I'll be fine. Can you take me home, please?" She hated the pleading in her voice, but she needed to sever all contact.

"If that's what you want." The concern in his voice matched the look on his face. He went into the bedroom and came back with his keys.

In the car, she was silent, sitting as close to the passenger door as possible, her gaze straight ahead until they pulled into her driveway. She was out of the car the second he stopped and bolted up the front steps. She flinched when his fingers brushed hers as he took the keys from her unsteady hand and unlocked the door. She squeezed her eyes closed. *Hang on another minute and he'll be gone.* If her composure would hold out that long.

"Katherine."

"Goodbye, Nick." She stepped inside and closed the door. She didn't slam it in his face in a show of finality this time. She didn't have the strength.

With legs as firm as water, she leaned against the door. Funny how the tears wouldn't come, now that no one else could see. She stayed there for a long time, letting the pain of a hope that was lost forever tear her heart to shreds.

Then the words Alice had said to her the morning they met were there, pulling her out of her misery. Helping her find her purpose. "Are you going to wait around and see if someone else steps in and does what needs doing? Or are you going to take charge and make sure it's done right?"

The burning ache in her chest changed to a searing jolt. She pulled herself up and took the stairs two at a time. Her briefcase was in her bedroom. She rummaged through the contents until she found the phone number she wanted. Then snatched the cordless phone from its cradle on her nightstand and punched in the number before she changed her mind.

"Corinne? Hi, it's Katherine Harper." She didn't give

the other woman time to respond. "Listen, I'm sorry to bother you on a Saturday, but I didn't want to wait another minute before I let you know my decision regarding the city council race."

Nick sat in Kat's driveway, staring at her front door. It stood as impenetrable as a vault door at Fort Knox. The ten inches between their seats in his car as he'd driven her home had seemed like a chasm ten miles wide. He visualized everything in his living room. Nothing there should have offended or upset her.

In frustrated anguish, he'd watched her struggle to put the key in the lock. She'd almost dropped it twice. It had ripped his heart out when she'd flinched away from his touch when he tried to help. No matter what he did or said, he hurt the one person he never wanted to cause any kind of pain. His plan had been to inject himself into her life a little at a time until she got used to him. Then she'd see how much he cared about her. But anytime he gained ground, it crumbled beneath his feet.

His first thought was to find Jeremy and seek his advice, but somehow Nick knew he needed to figure this latest problem out for himself. He closed his eyes and prayed. "Please God, I know I don't always do what makes you smile, but I honestly don't know where I went wrong this time. I didn't see her cry, but I know I've hurt her even worse than before. Show me how to fix this, or at least help me understand what's happening. Please, God." He opened his eyes and backed out of her drive.

At his apartment, the red message light was blinking on his answering machine. Not fit for conversation, he went into the kitchen in search of lunch. His breakfast had worn off during the game. He made a sandwich, but the light on the machine drew him like a beacon until he hit "play." His father's voice boomed into the room accusing him of trying to talk Katherine out of running for office.

Nick wasn't up for a fight with his father right now and if he called him, their conversation would turn into an argument. It always did. His father had his eyes on this council seat and he wouldn't let anything stand between Nick and winning the election. At the end of the message, the time stamp announced when the call had come in. Nick stopped on his way back to the kitchen and checked his watch.

"Aaaggghhh," he growled and hurled the sandwich at the garbage can. He grabbed his phone to call Katherine but paused. She wouldn't believe anything he said. His father had seen to that. This ended today!

The spot under the oak tree still had parallel ruts from where he'd parked his first car at his father's house. Nick climbed out and bounded up the steps. He jabbed his finger against the doorbell and kept it there. The ringing chime pealed incessantly throughout the massive house until his father snatched the door open with a snarl on his face for whoever had dared to be so demanding of him.

"Nick, what are you doing?" His father looked at him coldly before stepping aside so he could enter.

"I'm here to tell you that if you so much as say Katherine's name or even think it, I will withdraw from this election and won't allow my name to be printed on another ballot for as long as I live."

Edward turned to glare at him and left the door wide open. "What is it with that little do-gooder that makes you go stupid when you're around her?"

"That do-gooder," Nick ground out, "is one of the kindest, sweetest, most caring people I've ever met. And if you don't leave her alone, I won't speak to you again. I mean it

Dad. Leave. Her. Alone." The quiet intensity of his words held more steel than if he'd shouted them.

"What hold does she have over you? Don't you understand she and her background could keep you from reaching your goal?"

"What about her background? Because she grew up in foster care and lived in a children's home? She didn't kill her parents." Nick prowled the foyer like a lion with a thorn in his paw, itching to lash out at anything within striking distance before settling a contemptuous look on his father.

"I thought I was supposed to consider people for their accomplishments and shortcomings, not their parents."

"Since you're so friendly with that pastor, let me remind you, there's a scripture in the Bible about sins of the parents being visited on their children."

Nick stared at his father. Was his rationale that warped? "You honestly believe Katherine is responsible for her mother's death? That's crazy."

His father didn't dispute his question and Nick's hold on his temper snapped. "Then why don't I call the state attorney's office and we'll bring charges. Surely, I can get her convicted. Or why don't I go down to the police station and turn myself in for killing Mom. Never mind that the doctors said it was cancer. I'm sure she died because she carried me to term instead of seeking treatment earlier!" His entire body was numb. Because if he felt anything, he would have to feel the torment of not knowing a mother, and he didn't think he was strong enough to suffer all the pain that brought on along with this.

Edward stood frozen, staring at him as if he were a stranger. "Don't talk about your mother that way. And don't ever say anything about her in the same breath as that…" he sputtered.

"That sweet, beautiful, caring woman I'm in love with?" Nick filled in for him.

"You are not in love with her!" his father screamed. "You're doing this to get even with me for sending her away, aren't you?"

Nick's stomach clenched, squeezing the churning bile upwards until he felt it sear the back of his throat. He fought the urge to vomit. "You sent her away? My promise that I wouldn't see her again wasn't enough. You made her start over with strangers." No wonder she couldn't get past what he—no, what his father—had done to her.

"Son, now you know I would never do anything to intentionally hurt you. She was a distraction you couldn't afford. Remember how much you had going on. You had to retake your SATs because your math scores weren't high enough the first time," he said in a desperate scramble to justify his actions.

"My math scores? Well, here's a news flash for you, Dad. The only reason I scored high enough to get into the college you wanted me to attend was because that foster kid, as you keep referring to her, agreed to tutor me so I could pass the test. Without her, I wouldn't have gotten in." The blood that had burned hot and fast through his veins suddenly turned icy, sluggish.

"I think I hate you. I'm not supposed to, but God's going to have to let me commit this sin for now until I can stand the sight of you again." Nick turned and walked out of the open front door, slamming it shut and blocking out the image of his father. He couldn't get away from the evil in that house fast enough.

Nick gunned the engine when he pulled out into traffic, leaving a black line of rubber as tangible proof of his temper. The house he'd grown up in looked so foreign to him right now it could have belonged to a stranger. And if he was honest, it did. He pulled off the road and reached for his cell phone.

Jeremy answered on the second ring.

"Hey, Pastor. I could use a friend right now. One with a better vertical connection than I have."

"Are you driving?" Nick heard the concern in his voice.

"No, I'm sitting on the side of the road. I'll be there in ten minutes." He paused before he disconnected. "And Jeremy, thanks."

Jeremy was out in his front yard when Nick pulled up. He opened the car door for him before Nick got the engine turned off.

"What happened at lunch?"

"We didn't make it to lunch." He followed Jeremy up the sidewalk toward the front door.

"Why not? You both seemed fine when you left the gym."

Nick recapped what had happened and how pale and shaky Katherine had looked when he'd driven her home. "Knowing what I know now, no wonder she hates me." He hissed a hot breath through his teeth.

"She doesn't hate you, Nick."

He pinned his friend with a disbelieving glare. "She has every reason in the world to hate me. Whenever I come near her, I inflict some sort of pain. If not me, then my father and his perverse sense of protection over me." He paced, his misery and guilt driving his restlessness.

"I think the reason you hurt her is because her feelings for you run deeper than even she realizes."

"I might have believed you this morning, but not since I took her home." Nick pounded his fist on the bookshelf. "No matter what I do or say, I end up hurting her. I'm not running for city council. I'm going down to the elections office Monday morning and removing my name from the ballot."

"Don't do that. You said this has been your dream since you were a little kid. It won't solve anything if you pull out now. And it sounds more like you want to run away instead of fixing the problem."

"Running for public office was always my father's dream for me. He thought it would bring more power and influence to the Delaney name. I bought into it because I thought I could help people. And I thought he'd be proud of me. Now, I don't care what he thinks of me. I'm ashamed to have him as my father."

"Nick, you can't feel that way," Jeremy argued. "As upset as you were with him for trying to hold Katherine account-able for her mother's sins, you can't disown your father be-cause of his behavior. You are two separate people making your own choices in life. Granted, those choices sometimes affect the other because you're related. But that's the dif-ference between you and him. He only thinks of himself, whereas you think of others first."

"If I think of others, then why do I keep hurting Kat?" Nick asked. Confusion and a loss as to how to fix things gripped him by the throat.

"We only hurt the ones we love," Jeremy explained. "We try too hard and get overzealous in our attempts to please them and we forget to enjoy the small things that bring them happiness."

"I don't get what you mean by that."

"You love her. You're overeager and nervous when you talk to her. The wrong words fly out of your mouth and ruin your efforts. And she's sensitive where you're concerned. Maybe it's because she loves you, too."

Jeremy stopped him before he knocked his theory. "That's speculation on my part. I don't know for sure if she does or doesn't. She might not know herself. But you have a place in her heart and you'll have to treat her gently while you mend the rift your father has put between you. Dropping out of the race won't help, and this community needs someone like you. Stay in the race and pray. Ask God to guide your steps from here on out. Let Him lead you and your path will be blessed, whatever the direction."

Jeremy came up beside him, and clapped him on the shoulder. He said a prayer of peace and guidance over Nick before he let him leave. Nick drove home with a lighter heart than he thought possible since he'd walked into his living room to find Kat anxious and desperate to be anywhere but near him.

He took another shower, then fell back across his bed and stared at the ceiling. If he and God were going to talk about his life, and what needed work, he might as well turn his eyes in the right direction. Up.

The chime of the doorbell caused Katherine to put down her devotional. A glance at her watch made her wonder who would stop by this late on a Saturday night. She looked through the glass fan light before she opened the door.

"Jeremy, what brings you by?"

"Can I come in?"

The anguished look on his face brought her defenses up. "If you're here to plead for anyone with the last name of Delaney, I'm not up for it tonight."

"Katherine." Jeremy reached out and caught her arm before she turned away. "I'm not here for anyone but you. I did speak to Nick today after he argued with his father."

Her eye roll gained her a disapproving frown. "He doesn't know I'm here. I've been in prayer all afternoon, seeking God's guidance about what I'm supposed to do to help mend the hearts of two of my closest friends. I know what happened today and I know what you *think* happened. I knew you'd try to handle this alone. I care too much for you to let you face this by yourself."

She inhaled a deep breath and ignored the sudden wetness blurring her vision. "I thank you for your concern, but I'm fine."

He shook his head and walked past her into the living room, going straight to her couch and settling down as if he meant to stay for a while. "I don't believe you."

She stood in the doorway, stunned. "You don't believe me? Well, it doesn't matter. I'm fine. It'll take a lot more than a Delaney to hurt me. And just so you know, I'm running for city council. I can't allow Edward to gain a stronger hold on this community through Nick. Edward is a dishonest, manipulative person who would use his own son to con this community into giving him the power he craves."

Jeremy's mouth gaped open. "Katherine, don't do this. Not like this."

"Why? Do you believe Nick can say no to his father?"

"Don't enter the race because of anger or a thirst for vengeance. Seek God's will about what you should do."

"You're taking his side." Hurt tinged her words. "I knew you would." She launched herself from her chair as another act of betrayal from one more person she thought cared for her jabbed her heart. She should have known. "I think you should leave."

"I'm not leaving until you listen to reason." He stood and took a bracing stance. "I will not pick sides between the two of you. You and Nick can't mend this rift without God's help. I'm here to pray with you and convince you to seek God's wisdom and guidance in *all* the decisions you make. What you're facing now, the choices you make today, you'll have to live with the consequences of those choices for a long time. Please, let God lead you. Trust Him."

She lost the battle against her tears and they leaked from her tightly closed eyes. "Jeremy, they used me. Edward had me transferred. I can see now that Nick didn't know what his father had done. I want to trust Nick, but it's so hard. If his father is this diabolical, what's to say Nick isn't the same way? How can I trust him with the council seat between us?"

The dam holding back the disappointment, the disillusionment, all the wrenching pain of the past, broke. Jeremy listened as she told him about the letter Edward had written to send her away, what he'd said to her at the party and the phone message she'd overheard.

"Nick did it again. He let his dad convince him to use me so he could move ahead to that precious next level. But Edward's not getting away with it this time. The Delaneys may have beaten Kat Jenkins, but I'm Katherine Harper now. I know how to play their game. This time, I'm the one who's going to win." Her voice cracked with emotion.

Jeremy listened, rocking her while she sobbed out her promise of revenge. When she finally settled down, he led her over to the couch and sat down beside her. Still holding her hands, he prayed aloud, asking God to give him the words to say to help her see the truth. To find peace.

"Listen to yourself. Do you hear what you're saying? You want revenge. That isn't yours to take. That's God's right. Let Him deal with the deceit and the lies."

She tried to pull away, but he held her tighter, forcing her to listen to every word. "Your distrust of Nick is because of the things his father did to you. Each person is answerable for his or her own actions, not anyone else's. Edward Delaney holds it against you that your mother died, leaving you in foster care. And you're abandoning Nick because of the venom his father spewed on you.

"I know I'm supposed to tell you not to be angry, but I'm

human and what he's done to you makes me furious. But I have a responsibility for your soul, for the counsel I give you, so I'll ask you to do what I have to do, and that's pray unceasingly. God can take this ugliness and make something beautiful. We can't do that. Only God can." Jeremy released her hands and lifted her chin until her eyes met his. "Promise me you'll pray. That you'll diligently seek God's will in this decision to run for office. If it's what God wants, nothing can stop you, not even an army of Edward Delaneys. But as your friend, I have to tell you, Nick is hurting too. He wants to hate his father. He realized what he'd done today and they had a terrible fight, over you." Jeremy gave her a meaningful look. "That speaks of a man who cares about you. Treat his heart with more tenderness than he did yours in the past. You know what callous treatment feels like. Show God you've learned how to be gentle."

She wrapped her arms around him and squeezed, resting her face against his shoulder. "Thank you." She pulled away and stood up. "I can't promise I'll be able to put aside my resentment toward Edward, but I promise to ask God to guide me."

"That's the most important part. If God's guiding you, all the rest will fall into place."

"I've already told Corinne Hightower I'll run. There is so much more I can do to help the community in a position like that. Stopping Edward and his quest for power was just icing on the cake."

Jeremy stood. "I'll trust you to keep your promise and pray. I'll be praying too."

She walked him to the door. "Thank you for being my friend."

Chapter 10

After church on Sunday, Katherine stopped by Mrs. Tindle's house on her first follow-up visit to see how she and Stevie were getting along. Their house was a small A-frame with a fenced yard. It sported a tire swing dangling from a giant oak tree with zinnias and marigolds outlining the short sidewalk.

Stevie answered the door. "Miss Harper, hi. What are you doing here?" His grandmother came up behind him and scolded him for opening the door without waiting for her, then smiled when she spotted Katherine.

"Hello, dear. It's so nice to see you. Come in." She pulled the door wide and ushered Katherine inside, letting Stevie lead her by the hand into their small living room.

"I'm checking to see how the two of you are doing. I have to do some drop-ins and make sure everything's going smoothly for a while."

"I wanted to thank you for bringing Stevie to visit me while I was in the hospital. Seeing his sweet face made me want to hurry up and get well so I could come home and be with him."

Stevie left the adults talking. He lay on his tummy on the floor racing his cars around each other.

"I worried so much about him after the accident. I didn't know what would happen to him if I didn't get well. I'm all Stevie has. I thought about all the children who don't have anyone and what happens to them. It about broke my heart when they said Stevie would have to stay in a children's home until I recovered."

Reaching out a sympathetic hand, Katherine tried to soothe her anxiety. "But he did have you and you're together now. That's what matters."

"I know, but if you hadn't been there in the beginning, I don't think they would have considered letting him stay with me. You fought so hard against that caseworker pushing me to put him up for adoption."

"The important thing is you're together like you should be."

"What did you say to change her mind? She was adamant about taking him away from me."

Katherine hesitated. At the older woman's concerned expression, Katherine decided she deserved to know the truth. "When I was about Stevie's age, my parents were involved in a car accident. My father fell asleep at the wheel and they drifted into oncoming traffic. He died instantly. My mother spent three months in the hospital recovering from her injuries."

Mrs. Tindle gasped and pressed her hand to her chest. "You poor dear, I'm so sorry."

"I didn't have a grandmother, or anyone else. The state placed me in a children's home until my mother came home from the hospital. Because her injuries were so severe, they had kept her heavily medicated. When they released her, the doctors prescribed several pain medications. I guess, in her grief over losing my father, she abused them until she became addicted. When the caseworker stopped by on a routine visit, she found my mother passed out with the open bottles scattered on the nightstand beside her bed."

Staring at her hands in her lap, Katherine finished the story. "They immediately hauled me back to the children's home. I don't know if she ever sought help to overcome her problem and couldn't, or if she kept on using. A few months after I turned twelve, the caseworker told me she'd died."

She'd never shared this story with anyone but Alice. She'd wanted to tell Nick back in high school but hadn't been able to bring herself to say her mother hadn't loved her enough to stay with her. That she'd loved her husband so much she couldn't stand to go on living without him. Not even for her little girl.

"I didn't want Stevie to go through what I did. You two needed each other." Uncomfortable after sharing such a dark secret, Katherine gathered her purse, ready to leave. "I'll stop by once a month for the next six months. It's routine. If there's anything you need, any problem you have, let me know. There are programs and services out there that I can put you in contact with."

Mrs. Tindle followed her to the door. When Katherine turned to say goodbye to Stevie, Mrs. Tindle cupped her cheek. "You're a good girl. You'll make a wonderful mother."

She didn't know what to say. She poured all her energy into the ones in state custody. They were the ones who needed her. Besides, there wasn't a man on this earth she could entrust with her heart. Mrs. Tindle's words reassured her that what she did mattered. She made a difference in people's lives.

Early the next morning, Katherine sat in her office, working on a task list for her campaign launch while she waited for Gina to arrive. She'd spoken with Abby and arranged a power lunch for the afternoon, when they would brainstorm on a strategy for getting her name out there. After a long exhale, she readied herself for the leap into the deep sea of the unknown called politics.

Public relations and politics would be a challenge for a woman who prided herself on maintaining her privacy. Katherine had prayed about her choice, as she'd promised Jeremy, knowing God would have to head her campaign for her to have a chance at winning. She was as at peace with her decision as she could be. The *ka-thunk* of Gina's purse on the desk out front announced her arrival.

"I see you wanted to get an early start today." Gina came into Katherine's office with her coffee.

"They say the early bird gets the worm." Katherine smiled and delivered her news in a low-key, oh-by-the-way style. "Can you be on the lookout for a fax from Corinne? She said she'd send over the forms I need to get my name on the ballot."

"Really?" Gina squeaked. "I mean, you're really going to run? Go for the big prize? This is awesome. Have you told the judge?"

She swiveled in her chair and watched the excitement build, almost able to see the wheels turning in Gina's mind. "Nope. I'll let you have that honor since you spy for him anyway."

"I do not spy," Gina denied with vehemence.

"You tell him what I eat for lunch every day and then tattle if I don't drink all my milk like a good little girl. I'm thirty years old—I don't need a babysitter."

Gina gave her a squinted glare. "I worry about you, and so does the judge. We share information so we don't over-lap." She took her usual chair. "Seriously though, what made you decide to say yes?"

"I liked what Corinne said about helping the community." She met Gina's interested look with a straight face.

"Uh-huh. If that were all, you would have agreed before Corinne left here last week. Tell me what happened this weekend to help make up your mind."

"Why would something have to happen for me to decide this is what I want to do?"

Gina persisted. "No. Something had to have happened. Weren't you with Nick this weekend?"

"Nick has nothing to do with this."

"Okay, since I heard from Abby how Edward Delaney cornered you at the hospital dedication, does it have anything to do with him?" Gina was unwilling to let go until she had all the dirty details.

Katherine's eyes went wide before she got her expression under control. "I don't know what you mean."

"That translates to your change in plans definitely involves Daddy Delaney."

"Why do you have to give them such childish names?"

"Oh, no, you don't. I know a diversion tactic when I hear one. What happened?"

Katherine let out a huff of breath. "It wasn't only what Edward said at the dedication, it was some other things I realized this weekend. And I believe I can do a better job as a council member than Nick can. I really am doing this to help the community."

Gina looked at her as if she expected the word "truth" or "lie" to flash across her forehead at any time.

"I promise. Now, here's a list of calls I need you to make and a flyer I'd like to create that we can use as a mail-out. I'll know more after I have lunch with Abby and find out what she has in mind."

Gina reached for the list and the sample flyer on the desk between them. After a quick study, she offered Katherine a devious grin. "You said you kept that pack of crayons in your briefcase for the kids. Now I know the truth." She was laughing when she got up from her chair and left the room with the list and the flyer.

Everything after that was a blur. Katherine's morning was insane. She had taken several case files home with her for review over the weekend, but she hadn't gotten very far considering the emotional upheaval she'd experienced Saturday morning. She pulled out the files and dictated notes Gina would transcribe and forward to all involved parties.

She saved Stevie Mills's follow-up assessment for last. She wrestled with how to word her impressions in the file notes. There was the danger of developing an emotional attachment to the child. This was a two-edged sword. Not enough emotion and you didn't care about what was best for them. An advocate had to justify every recommendation they made with detached practicality while showing genuine concern for the child's well-being. It didn't matter that practicality wasn't the driving force behind her concern with this case. Her choices would stand up in an audit. Her passion to keep him with his grandmother was anything but detached. It was her childhood all over again. And that wasn't anyone's business.

At noon, Katherine sat in a booth at Dante's facing Abby, the strategizing for her campaign on hold until they finished their discussion regarding the eventful weekend.

"Jeremy agrees Edward Delaney should be tarred and feathered," Abby said.

"That isn't very charitable of our pastor."

Abby huffed. "It's what I want to do to him." She leaned forward. "Do you know how restrictive it is on my temper tantrums to spend time with a minister while trying to be myself?"

Katherine grabbed a napkin to wipe her mouth after she swallowed wrong. She fanned her face with her other hand. "Oh, my."

"Don't get too choked up. If Jeremy proposes, you're going to be my maid of honor and you know he'll want Nick as his best man."

That snapped her out of her teasing mood. "You wouldn't."

"I'm closer to you than any of my other friends. I will need you there lending me your strength. Of course, Jeremy has to fall madly in love with me first, so you're safe for five or ten years," Abby complained.

"You can use my campaign to keep you busy while you wait."

"This is true. Okay, here's what I've come up with so far. First, you have to file your intent to run. You need to do that by tomorrow. Do you have court Friday?"

"No, why?"

"Because Corinne said the Coalition is having a luncheon in your honor on Friday. They want you to speak." In answer to her surprise, Abby nodded. "I've been busy this morning."

"I'll say. What am I supposed to talk about at this luncheon, my very wise campaign manager?"

"This is your first appearance as a candidate. You should introduce yourself and talk about your plans for the community as a whole. Since the Businesswomen of Pemberly are hosting the luncheon, emphasize your ideas that target the business sector. It lets them know you consider them a vital part of your plans."

Katherine wrinkled her nose. "Do I have a speechwriter?"

"The best. You."

"But—"

"You'll be more comfortable using your own words. If you get stuck, use Gina. She's a great storyteller. She'll be an honest sounding board for you." Abby tapped her pen against her lip. "And, she'll be great at placating the reporters and fielding phone calls. She loves to organize and she can run interference, if necessary."

"You make it sound like I haven't been letting her reach her full potential."

"Nothing like that. Campaigning for an election is the busiest, craziest, most intense thing you'll ever do. Use the people you trust for as much of the work as you can. It'll mean you won't have to worry about the things they're handling."

"You're eating this up, aren't you?" She watched in awe as Abby ticked items off a long list she'd set on the table next to her plate.

"I separate myself from my dad's campaigns, but I know what they've tried that worked and what didn't."

They finished their lunch and Abby wrangled a promise from her to send over a rough draft of the speech by tomorrow.

"I have court this afternoon," Katherine said as they left the restaurant.

Abby stepped away, walking backwards toward her car. "Welcome to the big leagues. You can sleep *after* I get you elected."

Katherine was stuck in a traffic jam. She rushed into court and took her place with her files open, ready to proceed without a minute left. She kept her eyes off Nick, but sensed the weight of his stare. She wouldn't look. She wouldn't look. No matter what, she wouldn't look.

Ooh, she looked.

Their eyes met. He offered her a gentle smile. She snapped her gaze forward and didn't turn his way again.

"Miss Harper, kind of you to make time for us when you've had such an otherwise busy day." Was the judge glad she was entering the race or was that sarcasm?

"Your Honor, I would never let any political goals I might have interfere with my service to this court."

"I know you won't." And he gave her a speaking look.

"Kat, you're really going to go through with this?"

She glanced over at Nick. "I am. And it has nothing to do with you."

"Listen, we need to talk."

"No, we don't."

Thump. Thump. Thump. "Counselors, I realize you're now political adversaries outside my courtroom, but do I have to remind you we work *together* on the cases in front of us while we're here?"

"Sorry, Your Honor," they both mumbled.

As the hearing progressed, the mild level of tension between them grew until Katherine's nerves were wound as tight as a spring. When the tap of the gavel marked the end of session, Nick blocked her path before she could escape.

"I have to talk to you."

"No, you don't." She snatched up her briefcase and stepped around him.

"You can't run from me forever," he called to her retreating back.

By the time Katherine made it to her office, she couldn't remember why she'd agreed to this lunacy. They hadn't even started campaigning yet. She'd been going nonstop all day and still owed Abby a speech by tomorrow morning. Her head pounded in time with the thump of her heart, which was beating at a much faster pace, thanks to Nick and his threat.

Gina handed her a cup of hot tea. "Oh, thank you. You're the best." She took a sip on her way to her office, and then flopped into her chair with a groan.

"Think of this speech as something you'd say to the volunteers at one of the shelters you work with," Gina suggested. "Help them see what a difference they can make, or rather, explain what a difference you'll make on their behalf if they elect you."

She moved her hands away from her throbbing temples. "How did you know my stress is over writing the speech?"

The look of condescension Gina leveled on her was worthy of a queen. "I have been your assistant for five years. I think I know what you like to do and what you don't. Besides, Abby called and told me to nag you until you get it done."

After three starts, she was pleased with her results. Gina gave great advice. Katherine smiled with satisfaction as she read the last sentence aloud before going in search of Gina. This campaign stuff wasn't so bad after all.

Chapter 11

Friday morning, Katherine rolled out of bed already in prayer. "Please, Lord, let this day go well. Have me say only the words You give me."

She dressed in a cream pantsuit with a turquoise camisole. As she put her earrings on, the sun winked off the stones in the coat of her dog brooch. She reached for it. She'd worn it every day since Nick had pinned it on her jacket. With a steady hand, she fastened it to her lapel.

Abby picked her up an hour before they were due at the luncheon. She nodded her approval at Katherine's outfit. "The cream accents your complexion well. Cute brooch too. What kind of stones are those, colored diamonds?"

"Um, I don't think so." She smoothed the gold wire border with nervous fingers.

"Whatever they are, there's at least three carats there. Didn't you buy it?"

Katherine's cheeks heated, messing up the "perfect complexion" Abby had just praised. "It was a gift." A whimsical thing that shouldn't mean as much to her as she was afraid it did.

"I love it." Abby angled it into the light, making it glitter in the sunlight.

Desperate to distract her, Katherine picked up her purse. "We don't want to be late for my debut."

"That wouldn't be an ideal start to your campaign. I'll drive so if anything freaky happens I can take the blame."

"Practicing to take one for the team, are you?" Katherine joked.

At the luncheon, Abby sent Katherine to inspect her make-up with orders to hang low until she found Corinne and knew what the plans were. Abby returned in under five minutes without a smile.

Katherine went on immediate alert. "What?"

"Nothing. We're good. Corinne invited some reporters. She's using the luncheon to introduce all the candidates."

Katherine stopped cold. "There are only two. Nick and me."

"That's the two. Come on. You're going in there with a smile on your face and right after we eat, you'll give a speech that will blow their socks off." She hooked Katherine's arm in hers and propelled her forward.

Incredulous, Katherine dragged her feet. "You expect me to eat while the butterfly brigade is practicing loop-de-loops in my stomach *and* sit in a room with Nick Delaney, before I deliver my first speech to a roomful of prospective voters? Thanks for throwing me into the deep end without a life preserver." She took a calming breath, and sent a silent plea heavenward.

"If it's any consolation, Nick is sweating bullets too. At least you get to go first. Yours will be over sooner."

"I'll remember that while I'm forcing food past the lump in my throat."

As they neared the table, Abby said, "At least I warned you he's here. He won't know until you sit down beside him."

Katherine shot her a murderous look.

"Oops, forgot to mention the seating arrangements. Sorry."

"Dear Lord, please." Katherine moaned, hesitating before she took her seat. Beside Nick.

Nick glanced up, a look of surprise on his face. Then it was gone and he offered her a cheeky grin. "Hello, Kat. I've been trying to talk to you for a week and you've managed to avoid all my efforts. If I'd known attending a women's coalition luncheon guaranteed me your presence, I would have signed up earlier."

"Don't get any ideas. I'm only here because Corinne wanted me to use the coalition as a launching pad for my candidacy."

"Me too. Membership is down. She's hoping that together we'll earn the coalition more press coverage than if she featured only one of us."

"I don't like being used. I won't have my run treated like tabloid gossip."

Leaning close to her ear, he said, "Speaking of running, I wanted to talk to you about my father's horrible treatment of you."

She turned her head toward him. He was close. Their faces less than an inch apart. Awareness flared in his eyes and his gaze roamed her face before settling on her lips.

She didn't move. Didn't dare breathe. If she shifted at all, their noses—maybe even their lips—might touch. That would be bad. That could never happen. Ever. Very bad.

Nick pulled away and reached for his water glass.

The roll of his Adam's apple as he swallowed mesmerized her. She shook her head and dragged herself back to reality. "Can I ask you something?"

"Sure."

"The brooch. What type of stones are these?"

He smiled and shook his head. "Does it matter?"

"No. I mean, their color is perfect for his fur. Abby asked and I realized I didn't know."

He watched her finger the rows of stones while she waited for him to answer. "Champagne." At her crinkled brow, he leaned closer. "The color is called champagne."

"Why?"

"They're champagne diamonds. Four carats' worth."

He used his index finger to lift her chin back into place. "You deserve the best."

"I, uh…diamonds?" she squeaked. "I know it's horribly rude to ask how much you paid, but should it be insured?"

His laugh was rough and low. Velvet against sandpaper, sending shivers along her skin. "I took care of it. Just drop by Bergmann's every six months and let them check the settings and we're fine."

Now she was afraid to touch it. Shocked he'd spent so much on something she'd thought was a trinket. How he managed to infuriate and endear himself to her at the same time was one of the things she'd never understand about him or their tenuous relationship.

Moved by his generosity, it suddenly seemed important to explain part of why she'd entered the race. "I agreed to run for the council seat for a lot of reasons. I'm doing this so I can help the people of Pemberly. Jeremy said you're aware I overhead your father's message on your machine. I know you didn't have anything to do with it. But Nick, you have to realize there will never be anything more between us than an acquaintance. Our shared history is too volatile, too painful for me. We'd only end up disappointing each other. I don't want to hurt you any more than you want to hurt me. Let it go," she pleaded. "Let me go."

Corinne's presence at the podium and her subsequent introduction of the candidates killed any chance for further discussion. Katherine went first, thanking everyone for this opportunity to share a little about herself. Nick's speech ran almost parallel to hers. They both touched on business concerns targeted toward their audience and left the attendees with the impression both candidates had their best interests at heart.

After dessert was served, Nick asked, "Are you doing the follow-ups on the Mills case yourself?"

She set her forkful of key lime pie back on the plate. "Is that a problem?"

"It is if you're doing it to make sure the reports reflect things are going better than they really are."

"Excuse me?" He hadn't just questioned her integrity.

"Why are you taking such a personal interest in this case?"

"Maybe I don't like to see little boys ripped out of their grandmothers' arms by some overzealous social worker."

"I've read the file. Seen all the extra things you do for him that you don't do for the other kids assigned to you. I've heard it in your voice when you say his name. You know what problems it will create if you form a personal attachment to him. Are you sure there isn't more to your interest in this case than being thorough?"

"I'm not personally attached, and I am thorough. I'm making sure the caseworker doesn't have grounds to come in and suggest a relocation, that's all. Besides, you have less than two weeks left in family court before your sentence is up. Why all this extra interest in one of the kids now?"

He ignored her question. "I want him to be with his grandmother, too. I know being with family is the best place a child can grow up. But if he's too much for her to handle and something happens, you'll make it worse for them. The advocate's personal feelings can't influence the assessment. You have to remain neutral for the sake of their future together and your career."

"My career? You think I'm biased?"

"Normally I'd say no, but not in Stevie's case. You're overly protective of him. I'm trying to help you here."

She slapped her napkin on the table and reached for her purse. "I think I need to leave." Before she rose, she hitched her chin in challenge. "If you don't think I'm doing a fair job on Stevie's assessment, you go visit and do one of your own. You'll see how well he's doing living with his grandmother."

He laid his hand over hers where it rested on the back of her chair. "I'm sorry. I would never accuse you of being unprofessional."

She snatched her hand free and grabbed Abby's attention at the next table, motioning her head toward the door. Abby nodded and extracted herself from a conversation with two reporters. Katherine left with the feel of Nick's penetrating gaze boring holes into her back.

"Had all you can stand?" Abby asked when they pushed through the revolving door and stepped into the sunshine.

Katherine got in the car as soon as the valet pulled it around. "Nick Delaney and I become almost combustible when we deal with each other without benefit of a mediator."

Abby laughed. "I'm glad you understand the situation. Corinne wants to schedule a debate between the two of you. After hearing your speeches, I agree. You share similar visions for the city. Our objective is to show how much better your methods for achieving that vision are so people will pick you on Election Day."

"Nick and I don't share a similar anything. I wish everyone would stop lumping us together."

"Fat chance." Abby drove the rest of the way to Katherine's office in silence. "I have to run. I have a day job, too, with contracts to review for a couple of clients." With a serious expression, she rested a hand on Katherine's fore-arm. "You did well today. You could win this if that's what you really want, Katherine."

"I wouldn't have signed up if I didn't want to win."

After a long pause, Abby nodded. "Good."

Katherine walked into the office as Gina was putting her purse away. "While the cat's away the mouse will play."

Gina's head jerked up. Her eyes widened. "How was the luncheon? Did you sweet-talk each member of the coalition into making a huge contribution to your campaign fund?"

The strain of spending almost two hours sitting shoulder to shoulder with Nick had taken its toll. She took a seat on the small sofa in reception and let out a long sigh. "It wasn't a one-man show. I shared the podium with Nick Delaney."

"I bet that was fun."

"Not half as fun as sitting through the two-hour meal beforehand, smushed up against his big left shoulder. Did you know he's left-handed?"

"I do now," Gina deadpanned. "How did that happen?"

A little on the catty side after her bout with Nick, she returned in kind. "I believe you don't get to pick which hand you're more adept with. It happens naturally."

"Ha. Ha. You're a real riot sometimes. I meant, why was he there?"

"According to Abby, Corinne hoped it would give the luncheon more oomph if we both showed up and the whole tedious experience was witnessed by every reporter assigned to a news desk within a fifty-mile radius."

"You have to give Corinne credit. She's using your celebrity status and Nick's family name to breathe new life into the coalition."

"Are they that hard up for publicity?"

"No, but Corinne is a shark and she smells dinner. He's the most eligible bachelor in town, and you, my little pseudo-debutante, are on the fast track to becoming the city's newest sweetheart." She fluttered her eyelashes and draped her hand against her forehead in a mock swoon.

Katherine snorted and went into her office. "I'm the city's favorite redheaded orphan."

Gina followed on her heels. "You're quick to brush off all praise. Can't you let people like you? You're one of the kindest, most caring people I know. This city needs a thousand more like you. Give them a chance to see how great you are. If you do, I guarantee they'll hand you that council seat on a silver platter."

"Been looking into your crystal ball again?"

"No, I've been watching how you do at these public engagements you claim to dislike but blossom at. Just face it. You're the belle of the ball, Cinderella." Gina flounced out to her front desk.

Katherine sat staring at the case files on her desk. What was she really doing? She didn't belong in the limelight. She enjoyed working behind the scenes, being face-to-face with the people she helped. The idea of ruling from above wasn't for her.

She was so far out of her comfort zone, she couldn't decide if she liked it or not. The main downside to campaigning was the required up-close contact with Nick. They sparred and argued all day in the courtroom. They couldn't be together for ten minutes without growling or sniping at each other.

Their tutoring sessions had been the same in high school. No matter how she'd explained how to solve a problem, he'd argued there was another way—his way. She'd let him do it his way first, then laughed at his frustration when he plugged his answer in and it was wrong. She'd wait until he was through gnashing his teeth before showing him the right way—her way again. Oh, how he'd hated for her to be right. He'd never been mean or petty, just peeved when she understood the process better than he did.

If they stayed true to form, they would always approach a problem from different angles, testing their solutions against each other to see who was right.

Mrs. Tindle opened the door as far as the safety chain allowed. "May I help you?"

"My name's Nick Delaney. I worked with Miss Harper on Stevie's case." He held his identification up for her inspection.

The door closed in his face; then the deadbolt slid free and she opened the door. She squinted at the small print on his courthouse ID but stepped aside. "What can I do for you, Mr. Delaney?"

"Nick, please. I'm following up on Miss Harper's visit from last week." It was true. "Her report indicates everything is going well. I wanted to let you know we, or rather, the state and family services, are here for you should you need anything."

He looked around as she led him into the sitting room. There were toys strung in the corner with Legos and Hot Wheels cars and trucks lying on their sides on the window seat. The cushions were crooked on the couch, but Mrs. Tindle straightened them before she offered him a seat. "Can I get you anything?"

"No, thank you. I'm fine," he said and settled in on the couch. "How is Stevie adjusting to his new school? How are his grades?"

"He's doing fine. In fact, he earned a gold star on his spelling test last week. We've talked about discipline a little though. He gets restless in class and his teacher claims he distracts the other children. He's been doing better with that since I told him I wouldn't take him to the park to play with his friends if I received another bad report."

"That would do it for me." Nick approved of her method of disciple. "Does he show any interest in sports?"

"He likes baseball and soccer. But he hasn't asked about joining one of those community leagues. I'd sign him up if he did."

Nick came to his feet and paced. His mind worked better, faster, when he was in motion. He spun back around and faced her. "Mrs. Tindle, it's important to Katherine that you and Stevie stay together. I want to do whatever I can to ensure that happens. Is it too much for you to take care of him by yourself?"

Mrs. Tindle squared her shoulders and gave him an affronted look. "I know there are toys strung around this room, but I don't see how you can think I don't keep a clean house, Mr. Delaney."

The frosty formality of her tone warned him he wasn't saying this the way he should.

"I don't mean that at all. There are services the state offers that you might qualify for as Stevie's sole provider. I brought some of the brochures for you to look over." He set a stack on the coffee table. "They offer housekeeping assistance and there are trusts and civic organizations you can talk to about setting up a fund to cover Stevie's college tuition. If you lock in a rate now, he's guaranteed a four-year degree at a state school regardless of the current cost when he's old enough to attend."

"Why do you care about what I do to take care of Stevie and his future?"

He sat down beside her and met her direct gaze. "I care because I know how important it is to Katherine Harper that Stevie stays with you."

They sat in nervous silence for several minutes. "This

has nothing to do with the state or a caseworker, does it? You're worried Katherine is too attached to us and she might get into trouble."

"No. She's not in any trouble. I promise. This is about making sure Stevie has every opportunity to grow up with his family."

She nodded. "I thought when Katherine told me how she ended up in state care it was something she kept to herself. Obviously she's shared with you how similar hers and Stevie's life stories are."

Any doubt he'd had about knocking on Mrs. Tindle's door vanished. God had sent him here. The rest of this conversation would give him the answers to some very important questions about Katherine.

"She's suffered so many losses in her life. I care a great deal about her. She doesn't accept help very well. She's fiercely independent. I didn't realize her mother had been in an accident as well."

"Yes, the poor woman. That's how it all started. It's so sad and such a waste." With an obvious affection for Katherine and appreciation for her concern over Stevie, Mrs. Tindle told Nick the story Katherine had shared with her about how she'd lost both her parents separately at such a young age.

He fought the lump in his throat and the tightness in his chest. He understood Katherine well enough to know she would count her mother's rejection as her fault, and believe she wasn't worth loving. It was so clear to him now. It was as if God had pulled the curtain back and let the light of understanding shine on him.

The reason she worked nonstop, pouring herself into all those charities, trying to fill the void in other people's lives, was because she had this gaping hole in her own. She gave of herself, hoping that one day she would be good enough for someone to love her, to choose her over everything else. He shook his head. That silly, frustrating, amazing woman.

He made his decision. "Mrs. Tindle, thank you so much for seeing me today. Call the number on the back of any of the brochures there and they'll get your started with the process. If you have any problems, you have my card. Call me and I'll take care of whatever it is." He stood.

Mrs. Tindle escorted him to the door. "I appreciate you taking the time to bring this information by personally."

"I want to help make sure you and Stevie have what you need. He's important to Katherine. That makes him important to me."

"Are you going to marry her?" She smiled at his startled expression.

"I don't know. Right now she doesn't like me very much."

"If you let her see how much you love her, she might feel differently."

He couldn't find the words to reply. He nodded and left. On the drive back to his apartment, he mulled over the incidents in Katherine's life that had brought her to where she was today. He admired her courage and determination to succeed in a world that hadn't given her much of a chance to survive, much less excel.

At the last minute, he took the turn leading to the interstate and drove to his father's house. It was time they sat down and talked a few things over.

Chapter 12

His father greeted him with obvious apprehension. "Are you here to scream and tell me you hate me again?"

Keeping his expression neutral, Nick walked inside. "No, I want to talk to you. I need you to answer some questions." He gave him a hard look. "I expect you to tell me the complete truth."

"I'm known for a lot of things, but bald-faced lying isn't one of them." He spoke over his shoulder as he strode through the foyer and down the hall toward his study. "What do you want to know about Katherine?"

"How do you know I'm here about her?"

"Since the day you met her in high school you can't seem to get her out of your head. She is destined to remain the one thing we can never agree on."

"She is not a thing, Dad. She's—"

Edward threw up a hand as if unwilling to hearing more. "I know. She's the most beautiful, perfect, humble, generous, blah, blah, blah," he mimicked in a syrupy voice.

Nick's jaw clenched and he fought against his temper. "And you are the most pompous, arrogant, selfish, pain in the—"

His father arched an imperious brow at him. "I am. Your point?"

Letting out a frustrated growl, Nick paced the room, running a hand along the back of his neck. "What did you do to send her away?"

"Which time?" Edward asked, not looking repentant at all, which only added to Nick's dislike for the man whose blood coursed through his veins.

He shook his head. "It amazes me that we're related."

If he hadn't been watching, Nick would have missed the brief flash of pain that contorted his father's face. He masked his hurt quickly, but for that split second, it had been there.

"Tell me how you sent her away in high school," Nick demanded.

His father suddenly looked old, his shoulders forced down by an unseen weight. A weary edge tugged at his features. "I wrote a letter to an old friend asking him to transfer her to another high school, claiming it would give her a chance to dabble in paints before she aged out of the system." He heaved a resigned sigh. "Anyway, poof, she was gone, or so I thought, until she turned up in family court across the aisle from you."

"You can't play with people's lives like that. You're not God. You don't have the right to decide someone else's future."

"You didn't complain about how I arranged things for you to get into that fancy college or the money I've shelled out to make sure you're elected to this council seat."

"I'm not going to comment on the college part because I can't do anything to fix it now. But about the council seat, I'll tell you to your face so you don't hear it from someone else. I'm withdrawing from the race first thing Monday morning."

Nick watched the rosy tinge of mild temper fade into an ashen color on his father's face, then surge with red. He jumped to his feet and thrust himself in Nick's face. "Why would you throw away what you've worked for all your life? Is she really worth that much to you? Are you afraid that if you beat her she won't have anything to do with you?"

Then, just as fast, the rage ebbed and he slumped back into his chair. "Go ahead, take everything I've worked toward, everything I've done to secure your future and ruin it. It's only been my dream since you were a boy to see you on top. You would be a great leader, Nick. You draw people to you with your energy and enthusiasm. They respect you. It would be so easy to get you elected. Are you willing to let it all slip through your fingers over an orphan?"

"Dad, I want to serve in public office if I get the chance, but not at the expense of my happiness. If I win the election while I'm at odds with Katherine, I'll never be happy. I have to find a way to have her by my side, helping me, instead of running against me. Don't you see? If she wants this, I have to step aside. Holding a public office would be a job to me. It's not my life, Katherine is." He watched his father, but the blank expression on his face didn't change. "I wish you could see how good she is."

Edward moved away. He leaned beside the window, as if his legs couldn't hold him upright. He stared out at nothing.

It tore Nick apart to see him like this, but his father had created his own misery by being so cold and hurtful to others.

"I thought she'd take you away from me. That she'd tempt you with her smile and her sad life and you'd abandon your dreams. She had no ties here. I'd lost your mother. You're all I had left. I couldn't let myself care for anyone else but you." He looked back at Nick. "The first time you said her name, I knew. It was in your eyes. If she stayed, she'd take you away from me and I'd have nothing. No one."

Nick went to his side and rested his hand on his father's

shoulder. "You're my father. I'll always love you. But there's room in my heart for her, too. She was never a threat to you. She wanted someone to love her, but you sent her away. Do you have any idea how much your actions hurt her? How it made her feel? How it hurt me? I'm withdrawing from the race. Not to hurt you, but to show her I would make any sacrifice for her."

"Nick, please. There has to be another way. You're so close. This is what you've always wanted. You could have her and the election."

Halfway to the door, he turned and looked back at his father. "No, Dad, it's what *you* always wanted."

At home, Nick sat as the room darkened with the setting sun. His soul was beaten and bruised, his mind completely wrung out. He'd made the right decision. He owed it to Katherine to step aside. It was the least he could do after the way his father had treated her.

He called Jeremy. "What are you doing?"

"I'm getting ready for a date with Abby."

"A date?" Nick was surprised he could muster a smile. "I thought you were too chicken to ask her out."

"I am. She asked me. I took it as a sign from above. Why are you calling me on a Friday night?"

"I'm officially withdrawing from the race on Monday."

"Oh."

"I was expecting more from you. You're a preacher. I thought you were trained in eloquent wordiness."

Jeremy remained silent.

"Are you still there?"

"Uh, yeah, I'm here. You just threw me. Are you sure about this?"

He pressed back into the cushions and ran his hand over his face. "It's a long story, but yeah, I'm sure. Listen, I know you have plans, so don't worry about me. I'll buy lunch tomorrow after the game and tell you everything, okay?"

"Nick, I can call Abby and cancel. She'll understand."

"I'm good. I could use some time to myself right now. We'll talk after the game tomorrow." He opted to razz him about his date, wanting to lighten the mood. "Besides, I wouldn't dream of coming between you and your destiny."

"Funny." Then a long pause. "If you're sure you're okay to talk later."

Nick released a contented sigh. "I've never been surer of anything in my life."

Katherine set her purse on the table near her front door. Her keys hit the floor with a loud jangle. The loud peal of her house phone made her flinch. After an evening spent dishing out potluck at the soup kitchen for the homeless, she wanted to veg on the couch and not talk to anyone. She rushed to catch the call.

"Hello."

"Hi, dear. I'm not disturbing you, am I?"

"Mrs. Tindle? No, you're not disturbing me. Is everything okay? There's nothing wrong with Stevie, is there?" Immediate concern for the little boy wiped out her lethargy.

She leaned against a cabinet in the kitchen, listening while the older woman went on and on about how wonderful "that handsome Nick Delaney" was. She'd signed up to start Stevie's prepaid college fund. Another agency in one of brochures he'd left for her was sending someone weekly to help with the dusting and vacuuming.

Katherine rubbed her forehead to ease the tension pinpointed in the center while Mrs. Tindle explained about Nick's visit. Katherine mumbled her agreement that Nick was fabulous before they disconnected. She stumbled her way up the stairs and into the shower, trying to wake up.

That conversation had to have been a dream. She'd challenged Nick to perform his own assessment of Stevie's situation, not to become their champion.

The phone rang after she got out of the shower. This call had her sinking down on the bed.

"He did what?" She almost dropped the phone as the judge warned her of Nick's withdrawal from the election. "I'll be right there!"

She hit the End button with murderous intent before jumping into jeans and a sweater. Scraping her still-damp hair back into a ponytail, she came down the stairs, snagged her purse and scooped her keys up off the floor. The front door slammed closed behind her.

By sheer will and with some help from her cruise control, she didn't exceed the speed limit. A ticket was the last thing she needed right now. But blessed with a green light at every intersection, she made the drive across town in record time. Uncle Charles had the lights on when she parked next to a silver Mercedes and rushed inside.

The sight of Edward Delaney drinking from one of Aunt Melvia's antique floral china cups stopped her forward momentum. "I didn't know you had company."

"Come in, Katherine. We've been waiting for you."

Katherine blinked. Since when did Uncle Charles entertain Edward Delaney? "We?"

Edward stood and offered her his chair, then cleared his throat. "Katherine, I owe you several apologies. I know I have no right to expect that you will accept any of them, but it's important that I offer them regardless. My only excuse for the things I've done is that I love my son. I was afraid you'd take him away from me. It doesn't absolve me from what I've done or said to you in the past. I see now that I was wrong. I'm sorry for my selfish actions and the pain those actions caused you. You didn't deserve that kind of disregard."

She looked from one man to the other and waited for someone to tell her this was all a cruel joke. Neither one said anything. Instead, both men waited, as if they expected her to speak.

"Uh. Um. Hmm. What's going on here?"

"Katherine, dear, come have a seat. Melvia will bring you some coffee. Edward came to see me tonight hoping I would know how to convince Nick to stay in the race. It appears he's determined to quit and we don't know how to change his mind."

She let her uncle lead her to the chair Edward had offered her before.

"Why would he do something that stupid with the election so soon?"

Edward cleared his throat. "I'm not sure if what he told me was said in confidence or not, so I'm not comfortable revealing the specifics. Suffice it to say, he wants you to win the race."

A flicker of anger ignited low in her stomach, burning its way up her body, driving her to her feet, and bringing her numbed emotions back to a hypersensitive state. "He quit so I would win?"

"That's what he told me tonight."

"Of all the arrogant, asinine, patronizing…" She stopped mid-rant and leveled a cutting glare on Edward. "Why are you telling me this? Why are you really here?" Then, in a quiet, deliberate voice: "What do you want?"

At least he had the sense to look ashamed. He met her direct gaze.

"I need your help convincing Nick to stay in the race. I…" He glanced at the judge. "We believe you're the only person he'll listen to at this point."

She came forward until she stood toe to toe with the man who thought of her as something he scraped off the bottom of his shoe. "Give me one good reason why I should help you, of all people, with anything?"

He looked beaten, worse, frightened. "I don't have one." His voice was hoarse. "I don't even deserve your forgiveness, much less your help. But Nick does. I'm asking you to do this for him. If I keep carrying all this anger, I'm going to lose my son. He's all the family I have. I'd do anything for him. Even learn how to change. I want to be a better father than I am. I'm tackling the big stuff first. You're my first attempt at making amends. Of asking for help."

His words pulled at her, forcing her to remember verses from the Bible that she wanted to ignore, but couldn't. Not in her heart. *If you forgive men their trespasses, your heavenly father will also forgive you.* There was no escaping that truth, but she wanted to argue that Edward should have to work harder to gain her forgiveness. Have to do more than just ask. That wasn't what God required.

"He won't listen to me. He goes out of his way to irritate me, but he doesn't listen to me. I have no sway over Nick's decisions."

"You're wrong," Edward said in a quiet voice. "He's been paying attention to every word you say for over thirteen years."

She threw him a doubtful look, but caught a glint of pleading mingled with hope in his eyes. Every slight, every hurtful action he'd taken against her, bombarded her. Finally, she walked back toward him. "Just so we're clear, you're apologizing for the callous way you abused your authority when you were my advocate?" At his nod, she went on. "Are you apologizing so I'll help you convince Nick to stay in the race or do you really see you were wrong to treat a child entrusted to your care the way you treated me?"

His face flushed scarlet. "I'm ashamed of my behavior. Nick helped me realize how wrong I've been about you, about a lot of things." He met her gaze. "I have you to thank for Nick's improved math scores on his placement test. It took courage to overcome what you have had to, to become who you are. And I'm glad you care for my son."

Katherine stood in silence, absorbing the shock of his confession. The only way she could bear witness to her faith was to accept his apology. To trust God and let go of the pain this man had caused her. Jeremy assured her that once she let go of her past, she would be free to receive the blessings of love God intended for her. The promise of her heart's deepest desire gave her the courage to release a weight she'd carried for thirteen long and lonely years.

Proof of her obedience to God meant she didn't have to do this on her own. Trust God and be willing. She gritted her teeth and let out a long sigh. "Where is he?"

"I'm sure he went home. His emotions were running high when he left my house."

She walked out the door with as much determination as she'd entered. She gave in to a fit of temper as she pulled away from her uncle's house and gunned the engine. She was going to strangle Nick with her bare hands. How could a man be so… She couldn't even think of words to describe him and his behavior, and she was never at a loss for words.

Chapter 13

Three red lights on her way to his apartment complex didn't do anything to cool her temper. When she walked into the lobby, the bellman looked up. "Can I help you, ma'am?"

"I'm here to see Nick Delaney."

"Yes, ma'am. Is he expecting you?"

"He should be."

The man glanced down at his desk and scratched his head. "He didn't call down and let me know anyone was coming by."

She exhaled slowly to calm her raging blood pressure. There was no reason to subject an innocent bystander to the wrath meant for Nick—he deserved the full load. "My name is Katherine Harper. I'm Citizen of the Year and Mr. Delaney's number-one competition in the race for city council. We have each other on speed dial. Believe me, he'll see me." Her smile was feminine yet feral.

The man hesitated, then shrugged as if it wasn't worth the fight. Maybe she had more charm than she thought. He pointed her toward the bank of elevators and provided Nick's apartment number.

At his door, she pressed her finger to the buzzer and let it squawk until he responded.

"Who is it?"

"Why don't you open up and find out?"

He immediately snatched the door open with what she could only describe as a befuddled expression. "Katherine?"

"In the flesh, you egotistical, domineering, aggravating martyr wannabe."

"Huh?"

She pushed past him and stalked into the center of his living room. With her fists anchored on her hips, she leveled a menacing glare on him, ready for battle. "Are you crazy?"

He turned toward her with that look still on his face and asked in an infuriatingly calm voice, "Kat, what are you doing here?"

"What am I doing here? That's good. Like you don't know. I'm here because your father just informed me you plan to pull out of the election Monday morning. Is that true?"

"My father? When did you speak to my father?"

"Stop countering my questions with questions. I want answers and you're going to give them to me—right now." She threw her hands in the air and started pacing around the room. "You really intend to withdraw?"

"Yeah, I do. And what business is it of yours what I do?" He folded his arms across his chest in a defiant stance that made her bristle even more.

"If the reason you're chickening out is because you think you might hurt my feelings, it is definitely my business, Nicky Boy."

"What do you mean by Nicky Boy? And I'm not chickening out." His voice rose until it clashed with hers.

She rolled her eyes and gave him a patronizing scan

from head to toe with a doubtful smirk. "That's what it sounds like to me."

"Well, it's not." He growled and moved forward until he stood towering over her. "And frankly, I don't appreciate you storming your way in here at this time of night, yelling at me."

She straightened, bringing her face closer to his. "Got company?"

"No, I don't have company." Then, with an incredulous look on his face: "My dad really called you?"

She let out a long-suffering sigh. "Yep. After you told him you were wimping out, he went to see Uncle Charles. Their solution was to call me." She poked him in the chest with a sharp fingernail. "You can't quit."

"I can if I want to." He glared down at her.

"But why would you want to? You've always dreamed of going into politics. Now is the perfect time for you to do it. Are you afraid you'll lose to me?"

Apparently, the word "afraid" sparked the competitor in him. "No, I'm not afraid I'll lose to you!"

Sudden awareness of the warmth of his skin and the beat of his heart pulsing against her fingertip caught her off guard. She snatched her finger away from his chest. "Are you afraid you'll beat me and I'll be upset?"

He stepped away from her and dropped down on the couch. "Yes, I care about you. In fact, I care more about you than winning the election. If I have to choose, I'd rather lose the election than you."

His words wrapped around her in a gentle caress that cooled the heat of her temper as fast as a breeze after an unexpected spring shower. She sat down across from him in a suede recliner. "Well, I'd feel cheated if I won the seat because you withdrew. How could I be sure the voters really wanted me?" She fiddled with the magazine on his coffee table.

"There will be other council seats. I'll run next term."

"No," she argued. "You should run now. The city needs someone like you. You don't let yourself get bogged down in the here and now. You look at the big picture and find solutions for the long term. Pemberly needs that. They need you."

He gave her a lopsided smile. "Be careful, Counselor. You're giving me some good stuff to use in my campaign ads."

"Does that mean you'll use them against me and stay in the race?"

He exhaled a long breath. "I'll stay in the race. If I win, it's your fault," he warned, pointing a finger at her.

"Oh, I hope so. I really do." She paused in the doorway and winked. "I'll see you 'round." She walked out with her shoulders straight and her ponytail swinging.

He stared at the door after it closed behind her. This was the first time she'd made a grand exit that left *him* rattled instead of the windows. He leaned back on the sofa and closed his eyes. Slowly realization came and peace filled him. She didn't want him to quit. Why, he didn't know. But he'd stay in the race because it's what she wanted him to do.

At the basketball game the next morning, Nick was warming up with Jeremy. He lunged for an underthrown pass and caught a glimpse of shimmering black at the edge of the court. The ball sailed past him and he landed with a loud thud, sliding across the floor before he scrambled up with as much finesse as he could manage after having the wind knocked out of him. He sent a self-deprecating smile and a wave to Abby and Katherine where they stood gawking at his lack of grace.

Retrieving the ball he'd missed, Nick dribbled it as he walked over to them. "Good morning, ladies. Nice shirts." Their black T-shirts sported sparkling silver-colored rhinestones that spelled out P-a-n-t-h-e-r-s in big cursive script.

"These old things?" Abby pulled at her sleeve before giving Nick a sly smile.

Katherine didn't speak, but kept her eyes on him. Even though he directed his comments to Abby, his gaze rested on her. She squirmed under the obvious attention. "I couldn't find any pom-poms," she said with a straight face.

"Yeah, I've heard they're pretty scarce. I think the girls made their own." He maintained a somber face but couldn't hide the twinkle of mischief in his eyes.

Abby looked at Katherine. "Am I missing something?"

Katherine broke eye contact with him first. "Uh, no. It's just a little joke. Between us." Katherine turned to him. "So, ah, you're good this morning?"

"I'm great. I told Jeremy I slept like a baby."

"That's good."

Abby continued to eye the two of them curiously until Jeremy's arrival distracted her. Nick took advantage of the lull in conversation to test this new awareness he and Katherine had of each other. "I'm going to the Big Brothers Big Sisters banquet Monday night. Would you like to come with me?"

Before she could answer, he shifted the ball he held to his other hand and took hold of her arm to lead her away from the others. "I know you're going to the banquet, but would you like to go with me, as my date?" He held his breath, taking a leap of faith.

Instead of the "no" he thought she'd give him, she beamed a smile as bright as the sun. "I'd love to. I have to be there a little early for a sound check. If you can pick me up at five, that gives us plenty of time."

"Perfect." He dribbled the ball he'd been holding in his hand, but couldn't stop watching her nibble on her lower lip. With his mission accomplished, he needed to leave before she changed her mind. "I have to go warm up. I'm one of the starters."

She smiled again. "I know. Good luck. I'll be cheering for you—I mean, the team."

He walked away with a sloppy grin plastered on his face that matched hers. Yep, he was definitely growing on her.

The Monday session of family court was different. Katherine was used to frequent changes in counsel for the state, but she missed Nick. She caught herself looking across the aisle several times, expecting to see him. She admonished herself for moping and forced her attention back to the case they were discussing.

Mrs. Zimmerman didn't object to any of her suggestions. It made the hearing proceed much faster, yet time barely crept by. Katherine checked her watch every few minutes, going over her schedule for the afternoon in her head.

"Since we have a busy schedule on Thursday, I'm going to dismiss for the day. Both of you come prepared to discuss the audit Family Services has done on the list of files I ordered sent to your offices. Mrs. Zimmerman, I realize this is your first week in my court. If you have any questions, call my office and my clerk will assist you."

Katherine signaled her goodbye to the new woman with a nod of her head and rushed out the door. She had twenty minutes to make it across town or she'd be late for a meeting with Corinne Hightower and Abby. As she rushed out of the courthouse, she almost plowed into a man on his way inside. He caught her by her upper arms, bringing her to a halt right before she wiped her nose on his tie.

"Hey, where's the fire?" a familiar voice asked.

Glancing up, she offered a sheepish grin. Regaining her balance, she straightened her suit jacket. "Hello, Nick. Sorry about that."

"Where are you off to at full speed?"

"I—I have a meeting with Abby." She glanced at her watch and bit her lip. "I really have to go or I'll be late. I'm sorry." She squeezed his hand before she took off again. "But I'll see you in four hours."

He laughed and called out to her quickly retreating back, "That's three hours and forty-five minutes, Miss Harper."

Seeing Nick—no, running into Nick—was a good thing. She needed reassurance her decision was the right one and looking into those beautiful blue eyes worked. Now all she had to do was convince Abby and Corinne she knew what she was doing. Taking a deep breath, she opened the door leading into the reception area of Abby's office. Corinne was on the sofa flipping through a magazine. She looked up and smiled in greeting.

"Hello, Future Councilwoman. How was your day in court?"

Her greeting brought Katherine up short. "Aren't you getting ahead of yourself?"

"Oh no, I'm thinking positive. That's why I said 'Future' Councilwoman."

Katherine bobbed her head as if she understood. "Okay."

Abby breezed in through the glass door from the corridor. "Hi, ladies. I had a meeting down the hall and we ran over. Come on back."

Abby took her place behind her desk and motioned Katherine and Corinne to the two chairs facing her before she became all business. "Thanks for fitting this into your schedules. I know both of you are as busy as I am, but we really need to go over our campaign strategy since the election is in a few days."

"Abby, I want to thank you again for heading up Katherine's campaign," Corrine fawned. "You have a true knack for this. You should consider starting your own consulting firm."

Laughing, Abby shook her head. "I'm afraid not. If I did that, my father would insist I run his campaigns. He's a bear when he's on the campaign circuit."

Katherine sat quietly while the other two planned. She let them decide which aspects of the campaign required the most attention. Abby was the one who noticed her lack of input. "Katherine, this is your campaign. Feel free to speak up if you don't like something we've lined up for you."

"You two are doing fine. I'm just trying to take it all in."

Corrine prattled on with her day planner spread across Abby's desk while they agreed on a luncheon and a guest appearance on a local government news channel, and interviews with reporters from the newspaper. Katherine jotted down notes in a diary until Corrine slapped her calendar closed. "Well, ladies, as fun as this has been, I need to get started on arranging all these big ideas." She smiled, shook hands with Abby and patted Katherine on the back before she left.

Abby cocked her head to the side and eyed Katherine. "Want to tell me what's wrong?"

Katherine continued doodling on her notepad but peeked up through her lashes. "I don't know what you mean."

Responding with a snort, Abby rested her chin in her palm with her elbows propped on her desk. "For someone who wants to make such a difference in our little ol' town, you sure didn't give much input regarding the plans for what you'll have to do in order to be elected."

Katherine pressed her lips together and straightened in her chair. "Maybe I'm questioning if I'm the best person for the job."

Abby's expression changed from gentle concern to intrigue, and she scooted forward in her chair. "And *who* would be the best person, in your opinion?"

Her cheeks betrayed her with a heated blush, and Katherine shrugged.

"Uh-huh. I see."

"You always say that. What exactly do you see?"

"I see someone who's getting a little moon-eyed over her competition."

"I am not moon-eyed."

"Call it whatever you like. You sigh like one of the cheerleaders when he walks into the room."

"I do not. And besides, that would be the pot calling the kettle black, don't you think?" Katherine challenged.

"What do you mean?"

"Oh, come off it, Abby. You couldn't be more gaga over Jeremy if you two had been high school sweethearts."

Abby shook her head. "We discussed the finance budget during the entire drive home from the movie."

Katherine's conscience pricked her. "I'm sorry. I was teasing and I shouldn't have." She frowned. "I'm not qualified to give anyone relationship advice. I'm—well, I don't know what I am." She rose and moved about the room, coming to a halt beside a bookshelf near the window. What could she say that would express the gamut of emotions swirling inside her? Taking a deep breath, she turned toward Abby. "I don't feel the way I did about Nick, or even his father, anymore."

Then suddenly the frustration, confusion, admiration and love—yes, she couldn't deny it to herself anymore—welled up and poured out of her. "Did you know he put Stevie Mills's grandmother in touch with an organization that offers prepaid college funds and another one that provides housekeeping services to the elderly?"

Abby listened while nodding as if she understood at least part of the ramblings spouting from her mouth. But when Katherine paused for a breath, she asked, "Who is Stevie?"

Katherine reclaimed her chair and shared Stevie and Mrs. Tindle's story. "I mean, I was doing great avoiding Nick, not letting myself care about him. Then he had to go and do something like that." She waved her hands about in agitation. One came to rest on the brooch pinned to her jacket, sparking another bout of sharing.

"And this. You thought it was so pretty. Did you know they're champagne diamonds? Four carats of them. He had to have the thing insured and didn't tell me. I thought they were crystals." Her hands were clammy, her throat scratchy with fear. "Nobody gives a casual acquaintance four carats worth of diamonds."

Abby managed to get her mouth closed after a minute or two, obviously impressed with Nick's extravagance. "I'd say he thinks of you as a lot more than an acquaintance."

"But what exactly does he see me as?"

Abby shook her head. "You'd have to ask Nick."

"I can't ask him. He'd think I wanted to be more."

"Don't you?"

That brought her up short. Eyes wide, she gave Abby what had to be a deer-in-the-headlights look before she tried laughing off the question. Her attempt sounded more like a hysterical giggle. She leaned forward and rested her head on the desk. "When I agreed to run for city council it was because I thought his father could sway him into going along with his devious plans and the people of Pemberly would suffer from his lack of care. I can see now, from the things he's done for Stevie and how he applied himself in family court, that he'd be great as a council member. I never saw myself in public office. I'm happy doing my volunteer work behind the scenes."

Abby reached out and squeezed her hand. "If your heart isn't in running and you honestly think Nick is the better candidate, then we need to tell Corinne before she schedules all those public appearances."

"I know. But I feel like I'm letting everyone down. And Nick. Oh, I didn't even tell you what he tried to do Friday night."

"What?"

"He was going to withdraw from the race. For me."

"What?"

"He told me he was withdrawing from the race because he thought I wanted the seat and he wouldn't stand in my way."

"Oh, wow. Oh, my." Abby stood, struggling to piece together all of Katherine's disjointed ramblings. "You know what this means?"

When she shook her head, Abby explained. "He hasn't been looking for a debutante. He's been waiting for you."

"Me? What are you talking about?"

She tsked at Katherine's confusion. "You really don't have a clue, do you?"

"No, I have no idea what you're talking about. Tell me."

"The reason none of the eligible ladies of Pemberly have been the 'one' for Nick Delaney is because he's been comparing them to you. And it's obvious they've all fallen short." Abby grinned at her temporary speechlessness.

Katherine recovered soon enough. "Oh, he couldn't. I mean, he doesn't. You have to be wrong."

"I don't think so. Besides, why didn't he quit?"

She swallowed hard. "His father and Uncle Charles called me and told me what he planned to do."

Abby leaned forward, encouraging her with a look of open anticipation. "And?"

"And I was furious when his dad said the reason Nick

was dropping out was so I'd win. I went over there and well, I was mad. I—I—I beat on his door and forced my way inside. I yelled at him and called him chicken." She blushed, thinking how crazy she must have looked.

Abby was laughing so hard tears streamed down her face.

"What's so funny?"

"Oh, I can see it now." She was settling into giggles now. "The most eligible bachelor in Pemberly, known for his smooth disinterest in the women who throw themselves at him, has you, with the temperament of a Tasmanian devil, storming his apartment. I assume you got what you wanted since he didn't withdraw."

"He promised me he wouldn't quit."

"Do you love him?"

Katherine's eyes went wide at the directness of the question. "I don't know."

"Yeah, right." Abby pointed her toward the door. "I believe you have an honest to goodness date to prepare for with the guy you might be in love with. Now go."

Katherine hesitated. Abby didn't understand why this would never work. She didn't know the truth—Katherine's fear. She had to make Abby understand. "Every person I've ever let myself care for has left me. Either in death or they didn't want me. I'm not sure I know what love is or that I'm capable of risking my heart on it."

Abby wrapped her in a warm hug. "Talk to Jeremy. He knows about the most important love in the world."

Chapter 14

Somehow, Katherine managed to block out the last part of her chat with Abby while she dressed for the banquet. But when she opened her closet to decide what to wear for her date, the possibilities hit her, and she tried to calm her breathing before she hyperventilated. "Oh Lord, what am I doing?"

She'd never been on a date. She was thirty years old and going on what would be her first real date with... She wouldn't finish that thought either. Instead, she pulled out dresses in a rainbow of colors, studying each one with a critical eye before she settled on the classic little black dress. She slipped into the sheath dress and donned spiky high heels.

Her next decision, jewelry. There was no question about that, and she reached for the brooch. Four carats. It still made her stomach clench.

The doorbell chimed, snapping her back to reality. She hurried downstairs to the door and caught Nick tugging at the collar of the pale gray dress shirt that complemented his dark gray suit perfectly. In lieu of a hello, he offered her a clear plastic box tied with a satin ribbon.

She pulled the ribbon loose to reveal a lavender-orchid

wrist corsage. Her breath rushed out in a reverent sigh. "Oh."

She bit her lip to keep from saying anything stupid, or worse, crying. Instead, she stood on tiptoe and brushed his cheek with a feathery kiss. "Thank you."

He made her nervous. He stood scary close but didn't say anything. Her experience with this sort of thing was zero and since he bore the label of most eligible bachelor in town, she expected him to take the lead tonight. Why wasn't he saying anything?

His Adam's apple bobbed after a labored swallow. "You look beautiful."

"Thank you. I'm ready if you are."

He offered her his arm. "Your chariot awaits, my lady."

The banquet room at The Manor House was hosting the annual Big Brothers Big Sisters Appreciation Dinner. When Katherine walked in on Nick's arm, it set the entire room abuzz. People cast speculative glances their way when Nick escorted her across the room to where his father stood talking with Judge Pierce.

"Nick, Katherine. Are you pooling campaign resources?" Edward teased.

"Tonight isn't about the election." Nick looked down at Katherine and squeezed her waist where his hand still rested.

The heat of his touch warmed her skin through her dress. She struggled to understand the sudden increase in her pulse whenever he was this close to her. Hints of his aftershave teased her senses when he leaned in and spoke in a hushed whisper at her ear. A fresh, clean scent, reminiscent of spring and the crispness of the air when everything is abloom.

Corinne joined their circle of conversation, casting a

sharp eye toward Nick and his father. "Katherine, you really need to remember you and Nick aren't on the same team."

The flush of anger over the remark trailed from Katherine's neck to her face. "I guess you weren't here yet when we declared tonight off limits to campaigning."

Corinne waved her hand in a dismissive fashion. "You can't be serious."

"I am."

Corinne glanced from Judge Pierce to Edward and then Nick. She tried putting her comment off as a joke, but her half-laugh sounded strained. She reached for Katherine's arm. "Could I speak to you for a minute?"

At Nick's look of concern, Katherine smiled in reassurance. As soon as they were out of earshot, Katherine faced her. "Corinne, I meant it. Not tonight. We're here to honor an important cause. We can go back to campaigning tomorrow."

"Go back to it tomorrow? You don't get it, do you?" Corinne flounced over to a chair and motioned for her to join her. "Campaigning isn't something you do when you feel like it. You have to eat, sleep and breathe this race if you expect to beat Nick Delaney. The election is Tuesday. There are reporters here tonight, and it's free press." She cut her eyes back to where Nick stood talking to his father. "Although, showing up on your competition's arm was genius. You'll get exposure in both the political beat and the society page. I may have underestimated you. He doesn't have a clue, does he?"

Her temper spiked higher and higher with each word that tumbled out of Corinne's conniving mouth. "There's something I've been thinking about in regard to the campaign and you helped me see I've made the right decision."

Her words captured Corinne's complete attention. "Aren't you going to tell me?"

"Not tonight, no campaigning. You'll have to wait until tomorrow. Right now I've got a date to enjoy." She left Corinne to sputter her frustration over not knowing Katherine's plans for the election.

After the dinner, Nick drove her home and walked her to her front door. He waited while she unlocked it. Their actions were the same, but their motivations so different from the day of their lunch date fiasco. She turned to say good-night.

He reached out and pressed a gentle finger to her lips, stopping her words. "Thank you for coming with me. Sweet dreams." His lips brushed across her forehead, and then her eyelids and her cheeks like the silky wings of a butterfly. He walked to his car and drove away.

With the whirlwind of emotions churning inside her over her unfamiliar feelings for him and her decision about the election, Katherine doubted she'd fall asleep. But as soon as her head hit the pillow, she drifted off, suffused in peaceful warmth.

The alarm clock awoke her from a deep, restive sleep. She had tons of things she needed to accomplish today. At the office, she set a cup of Gina's favorite coffee in front of her.

"Is this a bribe?" Gina inhaled, savoring the caramel-sweet scent.

"Possibly. Tell me why Toby Hendricks was chatting you up last night."

Gina had raised the steaming cup to her lips and almost choked. "Um, how do you know who Toby is?"

"I asked first."

Blowing on her coffee to cool it, Gina sighed. "We've gone out a few times. But seriously, how do you know him?"

"The man has had his handy-dandy tape recorder stuck

in my face every time I'm at a public function since I was named Citizen of the Year. I know what newspaper he works for."

Tapping her fingers on Gina's desk, Katherine gave her an assessing look. "What is the deadline for a story to make it into the evening edition of the *Sentinel?*"

"Why do you want to know that? You have something newsworthy to share?"

Katherine put on her haughtiest expression. "I might. Can you call Toby and find out?"

"Sure, but I'll have to use something as bait."

"Tell him I can give him a story they'll run on the front page. Above the fold."

With an impressed arch of her brow, Gina picked up the phone and dialed. Toby volunteered to come right then, but Katherine held him off until the last minute to ensure there would be no leak. Five before noon, Gina led a suspicious but eager Toby into her office.

"Miss Harper," he said and offered his hand. "This is an odd request."

Motioning him to a chair, Katherine cocked her head and offered him a patient look. "Really? I would think that when someone knows something involving an upcoming election, the town would be very interested in hearing about it since the election is tomorrow. Any reporter would be thrilled at the chance for an exclusive."

With a wary glance, he cleared his throat. "Yes, but, you see, you didn't explain what that something is."

She straightened in her chair. "No, I guess I didn't. Forgive me for coming across as demanding while I outline a few things I'll need your assurance on before we proceed."

"It'll depend. My editor has final say in what goes in the paper."

"I understand. But you need to realize…" She leaned

forward, as if she was sharing a secret meant only for him
while seated in a room full of microphones. "I'm an attorney and I must have your assurance these small conces-
sions will be met before I'll tell you my story."

He watched her, trying to decide if she was bluffing or
not. He must've believed what she was offering was too
big to balk, because he nodded his agreement. "So, what
did I just agree to?"

She rewarded him with a pleased smile. "I'd like you
to title the article 'Why Nicholas Delaney Is the Best Man
for City Council.'"

He almost bit the eraser off the pencil he'd been tapping
against his bottom lip. "Excuse me? I thought he was your
number-one competition."

"Oh, he was. Until I realized he'd do a much better job
looking out for the city than I ever could."

"Huh?"

"Toby, I thought reporters asked who, what, where, when
and why."

"Normally we do. Miss Harper. This is a bizarre conversation we're having here."

"I know and I'm sorry for that. But this is the best way
to announce my withdrawal from the race. And I want to
make sure people know why."

"You're quitting today? The election's tomorrow."

"I know. But during my campaign, I've spent plenty of
time thinking about what this city needs and what we, as
citizens, have been doing to meet those needs. More importantly, I've thought about what I can do to help us at-
tain our goals more efficiently. In doing that, I've had a
chance to see Mr. Delaney in action. He has a great vision
of what to do and how. He doesn't only see the immediate problems facing our community. He's looking ahead,

thinking about what the choices we make today will mean to future generations."

Folding her arms on her desk, she willed Toby with all her might to see what she meant. "I tend to get bogged down in the 'here and now.' I do a lot of volunteer work. Most people think that makes me a perfect fit for public service, but it doesn't. I have to have one-on-one inter- action, directly helping people, or I'm not effective. Nick works better at planning and managing projects that affect numerous parties and he does it with ease and finesse."

Toby still looked doubtful. "You're telling me that on the day before the election you're withdrawing from the race and your reason is you think the guy you've been running against is better qualified than you?"

Could she blame him for not believing her? It was crazy. True, but crazy. "That pretty well sums it up."

"And I have your permission to quote you as saying he's the guy you'll be voting for tomorrow—that you trust your- self and the city to him?"

She met his speculative gaze with surety. "I trust my fu- ture to Nick Delaney with all my heart. You can use that as my quote."

After sneaking a quick glance at his watch, he grinned. "If I leave right now I should be able to get this typed up in time for my editor to yell 'stop the presses.'" He pumped her hand in an enthusiastic shake. "Thanks for making a dream of mine come true."

She laughed and watched him fly out of her office before picking up one of the case files she hadn't had time to give her full attention in these past few weeks. Taking a pleased breath, she got busy doing what she loved with a smile on her face and a warmth that reached her soul.

Katherine stayed at her desk until well after Gina had

left to dictate notes on several files that were pending. As she shut her computer down, the phone rang.

"Katherine Harper."

"I can't believe you. How could you do this to me? I made you!" Corinne screeched in her ear.

"I didn't do anything to you, Corinne, and the last time I read my Bible it said God made me." Her tone underscored with steel. "Now, if you'll calm down, I'll talk to you. Otherwise, we have nothing to say to each other."

"This is what you meant at the dinner the other night, isn't it?"

"Yes, it is. I'd thought about dropping out and after you kept on about plotting and scheming, I realized you thought I would owe you if I won the election. I have no interest in blackmail or feeling beholden to anyone. If I'd won, it would've been because the people of Pemberly thought I had their best interests at heart. Which, by withdrawing and supporting Nick, I do. He's the perfect person to serve on the council. Once you calm down, you'll realize that."

"I know how his father works. He convinced Nick to suck up to you to gain your trust. But you're wrong. With the council seat in his hand you'll find out Nick Delaney doesn't have a reason in the world to show up on your doorstep."

"That may be true, but I had to do what I thought was right, and this is right for me."

"Fine, but don't say I didn't warn you when you're sitting home alone every Friday night while he's grabbing photo ops with some other woman." After that parting jibe, Corrine hung up.

Katherine sat for a few minutes worrying over Corrine's words. *Stop it.* She couldn't account for anyone else's actions but her own. If this were part of God's plan for her life, it would happen. If not, at least she'd taken the high road. At peace, she turned off her desk lamp before picking up her briefcase. She locked her door and headed home.

As she pulled into her driveway, the blood roared in her ears and she let out a small squeal. Swinging on her porch swing was none other than Nick Delaney. She closed her eyes and took small even breaths before she climbed out of the car, firm in her belief that Corinne Hightower was a complete idiot.

"Hi."

"Hello. How was your day?" He used his foot to stop the swing.

She worried her lip with her teeth before stepping up onto the porch and into the light. "Good and yours?"

"Ehh." He shrugged. "The morning was boring. I spent hours reading briefs and depositions. But then around one o'clock, *The Sentinel* sent Toby Hendricks over with a copy of an article slated for their evening edition. They wanted to run my opinion of a story on the front page of tomorrow's morning edition. Imagine my surprise when I found my name spelled out in the headline?"

"Oh? Should I complain that they're showing favoritism the day of the election by giving you extra press?"

He stood and paced the confines of the small porch. "Why?"

"Why what?" Until she knew how he felt about what she'd done, she wasn't giving him anything to use against her.

He shot her an impatient glare. "Don't try that. Why did you withdraw—the night before the election?"

"Did you read the story? It's all there in black and white."

"I read the article. In fact, I read it ten times. Are you doing this because you think I really want to win that bad?"

"Nick, you wouldn't have run if you didn't want to win."

"You know what I mean. Did you withdraw because I was going to withdraw for you?"

"No, I withdrew because I entered the race partly to get even with your father and that was wrong. I've never had any interest in politics as a career. I prefer my volunteer work. You've worked and prepared for this your whole life. I didn't want to risk people voting for me because of my volunteer work and the Citizen award. This was the best way."

"You think it's best because it's too late for me to withdraw."

"You're not withdrawing." She folded her arms across her chest, ready to argue. "You're going to win and accept the nomination. And years from now, you'll be governor or maybe a senator, and then, who knows, maybe president. You were meant to serve. I did it this way to keep you from ruining your chance at fulfilling your destiny."

A muffled whimper caught her attention. She turned toward the far side of the porch and spotted a large basket with a blue bow tied to the handle. "What's that?"

"I brought you a present."

She reached up and touched the brooch pinned to her scarf. "I believe you've already given me a nice enough gift to cover years' worth of future obligations."

"Nah, this one's to help me out."

She waited while he walked over to the basket. He squatted down and quirked his lips into a lopsided grin. "Trust me."

"I've heard that before."

He pulled the blanket back and up sprang a golden head with chocolate brown eyes.

"Oh, he's precious." She was on her knees in front of the basket before Nick could lift the puppy out of its nest.

"How do you know it's a he?"

She pointed to the bow. "Blue ribbon."

"Oh, yeah, that. Okay, so you pay attention to details."

The puppy snuggled against her while she held him in her lap. He had a sparkly collar around his neck.

"I told you I'm not home enough to take care of a puppy." She wanted to be upset with him. Her emotions were a mess and he wasn't playing fair. But this little guy was too cute for her to stay mad.

"I know, but he needs a good home. I can't keep him at my apartment so we need a new place to stay."

"We? Don't you mean 'he'?"

"No, I mean us. We're a package deal."

Her head spun and the world tipped. The frantic beat of her heart drummed in her ears. "A package deal?" The words as soft as a vapor in the wind.

Nick sat down next to her and scratched the puppy behind the ears. "You can't always be here to feed him or walk him. I can help. You know, coordinate my schedule so I get home early when you're working late or out volunteering."

All teasing left her mind. She wanted—no, she needed—him to spell out exactly what he meant. He must have understood her need, because he reached down and tugged something from the dog's glistening collar.

Looped through the ribbon was a ring. A ring with a huge emerald-cut diamond and baguettes running down the sides of the band. "This was my mother's." Nick cleared his throat and his voice dipped to a reverent tone. "My father gave it to me yesterday thinking I might have a better place to keep it than his wall safe."

Katherine felt the burn of tears but blinked to hold them back. She didn't want anything distorting her view of his beautiful blues eyes as his gaze rested on her in what she recognized now as the color of love.

Nick took her left hand and poised the ring at the tip of her third finger. "I think it would look really nice right here for the next sixty or seventy years." He looked at her expectantly.

A single tear slid down her cheek, dislodged from the shimmering pool in her eyes when she nodded her head in agreement. He slipped the ring past her knuckle with ease before he bent his head and pressed a kiss over its new home.

"I love you. I've always loved you, Katherine Jenkins Harper. I'll spend the rest of my life showing you how much I love you if you say you'll marry me."

Wrapped in Nick's embrace, her face pressed against his shoulder, her answer was muffled but distinct. "Yes."

Drawing back, she gazed into his eyes, wanting to share the wealth of happiness bubbling up inside of her. "I love you, too. I think I always have."

Placing the puppy back in his basket, Nick stood. Holding on to her hand, he pulled her up. He slid his fingers through her hair and lowered his mouth to hers. The touch of his lips was warm and tender. A sense of belonging settled over her as his arms encircled her, drawing her against his heart. She breathed in the joy of coming home.

* * * * *